F*ck Me Daddy
A Port Canyon Chronicle

Kinsley Kincaid

Copyright © 2025 by Kinsley Kincaid

All rights reserved.

No part of this book may be reproduced in any form or by any electronic or mechanical means, including information storage and retrieval systems, without written permission from the author, except for the use of brief quotations in a book review.

ISBN eBook: 978-1-998646-16-6

ISBN Paperback: 978-1-998646-17-3

Cover Design: Ashes and Vellichor Designs

Editing: Rumi Khan

Proofreading: N.J. Weeks

fingers crossed

I feel a Pulitzer Prize in my future with this one.

Playlist

I Love You, I'm Sorry - Gracie Abrams
NDA - Billie Eilish
How Bad Do You Want Me - Lady Gaga
Guys My Age - Hey Violet
Wood - Taylor Swift
See You Again (feat. Charlie Puth) - Wiz Khalifa
Kitty Kat - Megan Thee Stallion
Abracadabra - Lady Gaga
Paris - Taylor Swift
Captain Hook - Megan Thee Stallion

Disclaimer

Please be aware this book contains many **dark themes** and subjects that may be uncomfortable/unsuitable for some readers. This book contains **heavy themes** throughout. Please keep this in mind when entering F*ck Me Daddy; A Port Canyon Chronicle. Content warnings are listed on authors' social pages & website.

This book and its contents are entirely a work of fiction. Any resemblance or similarities to names, characters, organizations, places, events, incidents, or real people are entirely coincidental or used fictitiously. If you find any genuine errors, please reach out to the author directly to correct it.

Thank you.

Please do not distribute this material. It is a criminal offence!
This book is intended for 18+ only.

Note from Kins

My loves.
My little bats and queens.
You all have been so incredible waiting for this baby. To find out, who is Harper's Daddy? Has left you in suspense for over two years. Good news, if you keep reading all will be revealed, finally, I know. But in fairness, I knew the entire time, but I get it. Keeping a secret for this long isn't nice. I hope this story is an acceptable peace offering, because I must admit,
I kind of love it... a lot!

Before you flip the page

I also come with a personal update!
I am so sorry to report that I've yet to be fucked by a ghost. So once again, all sexual parts & acts are strictly my interpretation of what I believe it would be like to fuck a ghost.
BUT I did choke on my own spit plenty while writing this baby. Which leads me to believe I have now been tonsil hockey'd by one!
Progress baby!! How exciting! But still no penetration.
Let us not dwell on the could-have-beens, and celebrate the what has.
Okay, enough about getting ghost dicked.
Go immerse yourself back into Port Canyon and enjoy the ride!
xx kins

Port Canyon

Isolated deep within the wild mountains of Washington State, Port Canyon is very much like most historic towns; cobblestone roadways lined with natural stone-front shops and a rustic clock tower features prominently in the town square. Relatively untouched by modernization, many of its buildings are unchanged since it was first settled in the 1800s. Filled with Victorian castle-like estates, some decorated in a dark gothic style, and completed by brightly light cottages covered in vines. Nothing about Port Canyon is new, less than nothing about it is normal.

Outside of Halloween, you will rarely find visitors roaming the town. New residents are few and far between, until Fallon arrived. She has cemented her legacy into Port Canyon and its history only making the town even more magical.

Although, this version, this perspective and journey focuses on Harper Hayes, Fallon's best friend and the Mortician family. She has been preparing to take over her family's responsibility since birth and has thrived knowing so. Even through tragedy, Harper has always been able to see the light and turned her grief into drive. Her passion for the afterlife and continued care of the newly dead is simply romantic. The legends, legacy and responsibility are embedded into her heart and soul. Harper takes pride in playing a part in the dead transitioning into their afterlife, despite the oddities her father has developed throughout the years. He has become a myth all in his own.

The other founding families who call Port Canyon home are very protective of their secluded little town. They are the ones who keep the legacies and legends alive. You will briefly meet some here, although this is not their story. This is the story of the mortician's daughter and her familys legacy past, present and future.

The Mortician's abode is where this story calls home.

There will definitely be ghosts, plenty of banter and tons of the fucked-up shit we love.

Welcome Back to Port Canyon.

Harper
Prologue

You have spunk.
You're just so bubbly and happy, all the time.
Go away, Harper, you're so fucking annoying.
Harper, your dad's a fucking freak.
Harper, just stop!
You are not worthy. You will never be good enough.
The mask I wear hides the hurt.
My aura is a facade.
I miss my mom.

Screaming in the middle of the deserted highway, on the same bridge Merrick died driving off of, I wait with arms wide in the dead of night.

Tourists travel down the narrow road, often trying to enter when it's forbidden. Someone is bound to come, eventually.

The damp air chills me.

Goosebumps form along my flesh.

The distant roar of an engine excites me.

The driver revs it as they take the twists and turns between the tree-lined mountains.

Echoes get louder.

Adrenaline ignites.

It's coming.

Whispering to my dad, the mist of my breath evaporates into the sky and I hope he can hear me in his sleep. "I love you, I'm sorry."

Now, you're probably wondering how we got here. Playing a game of chicken with a moving vehicle.

I would be too, if I were you.

But I am me, and, unfortunately, I know exactly how this came to be. And, for the record, I'm not depressed. Well, maybe I am a little. It would make sense considering the current circumstances. But a part of me is yearning to feel alive. I've numbed myself for so long to the chatter of those who don't get me and just assume. And finally, my mind is ready to feel and fly.

But back to what started it all. Brace yourselves, because even I was fucking alarmed by it at first.

Now picture this: you're getting ready to accept a new body in your basement morgue. Casually, with giant noise-canceling headphones on, you're walking down the narrow white staircase. Then, just as you turn the corner, time freezes and you see shit you can never unsee. Your heart drops into the pit of your stomach, and the once pounding bass erupting your eardrums is silent. Because all your focus and attention has moved to the one life-changing moment before you.

Turning around, your feet hurry up the stairs, fingers brush against the cool metal rail, reminding you that this is real. You are not dreaming. Panting, the door closes once you reach the main level. Your body collapses, mortified and confused. And from that day on, every time you close your eyes, it's all you see. So, you spend your nights in the graveyard across the street, evading sleep and the reality of what life has become.

Without going into the graphic details, just yet, I believe it's safe to say that you'd be pretty fucked up too, if you caught your dad fucking your dead mom's corpse in your childhood home and place of business.

The same corpse which he had religiously tried to maintain since her passing.

But we will get to all of that later. Don't worry, because you need to know everything. From how we got from that, to this extreme. Perhaps some reflection before the end would be helpful for me too.

Until then, enjoy me taking this bridge for myself.

My name will live here, along with my legend and legacy.

And knowing this will piss off my best friend's baby daddy, Merrick, tops the cake. The guy thrives on attention and dramatics. And since he is already dead, there is no way he can top this. He's going to be so pissed and I couldn't be more excited.

What a time to be alive... for now.

The roar of the engine gets louder, echoing between ridged mountains and green pines. Eyes close in anticipation. I left a journal for Fallon to find, explaining everything over my years of life, should I lose this vicious game. She'll understand once she reads it. I hope.

I can faintly hear the howling of people as the car approaches. Idiots who think driving at high speeds will break the barrier protecting Port Canyon from the rest of the world.

It won't.

The town will reject them. The car will crash like it just hit a brick wall. And my father will have new bodies to prepare by sunrise.

Waves crash on the rocks below. The still cool air is now blowing aggressively. And the town and I prepare. Relaxing my body, I take a final deep breath, my lungs fill, pushing on my rib cage. A loud horn honking follows, and I exhale steadily through my nose. I am unbothered. Through my eyelids, the bright headlights disturb the darkness I have been enjoying.

Tires squeal against the bridge's flat top. The driver attempts to brake before it's too late, and they take me, before taking themselves.

My brain expects the impact to occur within seconds. I count down in my head, *three, two... one.*

One comes, and I'm hit from the side. The impact knocks the wind out of me and my feet fly off the ground. My body feels ice cold as it moves through the air. My mind wonders if this is what it's like to die. Is everything moving in slow motion so you can absorb everything before it all ends? At least it doesn't hurt.

And as that thought leaves me, my body collides with the hard ground. Damp grass sticks to my cheek and my head bounces, giving me whiplash. Reaching up, the back of my hand wipes the fallen hair off my face. Looking up, I attempt to get my bearings, but I am stunned speechless. Everything just got a million times more complicated.

Fuck me.

And for the record, what led me here, tonight, was more than what I saw my dad doing that day. This goes a lot deeper.

And to fully understand the chain of events bringing us to the bridge tonight, you need to start at the beginning.

So, shall we?

1. Harper

Reading through my journal, childhood memories flood through my mind. The stained parchment flips loudly under my fingers.

Memories I cherish and others I wish would disappear. And temporarily they do. Because the sound of sweet giggles and tiny footsteps pull my attention. Quickly, I close the book and slide it back under my bed. And just in time, because from the corner of my eye I catch a glimpse of cute wavy white hair peeking around the corner of the doorframe.

Sitting up straight with crossed legs, I hold my arms out long and the biggest smile adorns my face. "Come here, sweet girl," I encourage.

Chunky toddler legs waddle toward me. She is

wearing only a pair of her big girl underwear, with her bold and beautiful hazel eyes focused on me, Aunty Harper.

Hailey jumps, and I wrap my arms around her, bringing her close.

Truly, nothing is better than the warm embrace of your two-year-old niece. Her tiny arms squeeze around my neck as I inhale her scent of baby lotion and fresh air.

"Hailey Knight, get that cute tooshie over here," Fallon jokes, trailing behind with her pregnant belly. Baby number two is due anytime now, and it's a girl. Fallon intends to name her Lottie. And I cannot wait to meet her!

Hailey looks identical to her father, but is more reserved, introverted, observant. She sees and knows all. Wisdom flows through her, and I am excited to see where she takes it. And she keeps Merrick on his toes with her sass and eye rolls. Which brings me immense amusement.

"And what do I owe this great pleasure?" I ask, intrigued. Fallon is my best friend, who also lives across the street from me. She takes care of the graveyard and assists with spirits transitioning, helping them adjust without pressure and keeping their afterlife peaceful. But before they get to her, I prepare the bodies. It's a job I have taken more responsibility for over the years. As my father gets older, he is stepping back. Because soon, I will be the head mortician. The Hayes family has been responsible for this duty since the founding of Port Canyon hundreds of years ago. It's a task I do not take lightly. It's an honor I love.

Hailey stays tucked into me as my dad's loud voice interrupts, "Honey, we have two fresh ones coming in tonight. Fallon, we'll call you once they are ready."

Fallon, who is in sweatpants, Converse, and a tee, brushes her dark hair back, blowing out a sigh, before yelling back, "Thank you."

I mouth *sorry* to my best friend. My heart sinks for her, she's exhausted.

The closer to October we get, the more chaotic our duties become. Outsiders think we are full of shit, which they later find out as an inaccurate assumption. Because regardless of their futile attempts, Port Canyon will not let you in. And most end up dying from trying. So, I suppose they get what they came for, a one-way ticket in.

If they would wait until the beginning of October, it would be a non-issue, but kids will be kids. Their frontal lobe is underdeveloped and common sense doesn't exist and therefore death isn't a probability in their little heads, but it is, so here we are. More bodies to prepare and more spirits to support as they cross over.

"Hails wanted to see Harp-Harp." Fallon smiles with pride, hiding the stress behind her eyes as she watches her kid snuggle into my neck. Fingers play with her hair, and my lips whisper against Hailey's head, "How did you know I needed to see you, too?"

Her father is an asshole, but I could never hold that against this cutie. I chuckle subtly.

Fallon rubs her stomach. "Come on Hails, Harp-Harp has work to do and you have a bed calling your name back at home." Sleep evades her the further along she's gotten into her pregnancy. It's the extreme discomfort my bestie cannot escape.

"I love you, sweet girl." I squeeze Hails once more before letting her go. Her tiny lips kiss my cheek and instantly my heart becomes full.

A child's love is unconditional. Not yet tampered with by the real world.

"Love you, Harp-Harp." Her words melt me. I adore this little girl.

Jumping out of my lap, she rushes out of my bedroom doorway and passes her mom, who rolls her eyes. "This kid is either full steam ahead or impossible to get going. She doesn't have any other setting." Fallon blows out a deep breath before turning on her heel, blowing out a deep sigh. "Text me later. I'll be up."

I shake my head. "Please try resting. I hate seeing you like this."

Fallon waves her hand at me as she walks away.

I hear the front door creek open, then close shut, before allowing my body to fall back on the plush white area rug that lays atop the dark wood, relaxing my mind and body before the storm of corpses arrives.

Flames flicker in the stone white fireplace, where bunches of pink roses decorate it. Every few days I go into our massive garden and cut them fresh, just as my mom did years ago when she was still here with me.

Shadows of flickering flames and swaying trees dance against the white wall layered in intricate molding, with my room dimly lit. It's beautiful. Shining bright for the last time, until the next full moon, I admire its beauty and remember its meaning. The brief escape from my mind is over. Dad is passing the torch, so to speak, to me, this October. The next full moon signals the ceremony, something so incredibly sacred to us founding families. But as years of discussion become reality, I am questioning my entire existence. Who am I outside of this life? Am I the most authentic version of myself?

I do so much to escape, to be anywhere else, but

have I ever lived? That bothers me the most. It's the one question which is continuously on repeat. These thoughts terrify me. I am the bubbly one, the best friend, the doting daughter and aunt. The unsuspecting one, struggling to come to terms with reality now that it is about to hit me right in the face.

Is this what people call 'cold feet'?

Oh my, am I the terrified midlife crisis bride in this scenario?

How fucking annoying!

Shaking my head against the rug, I snap out of this free fall. The crackling of the wood centers me, and my eyes drift shut. The tips of my fingers tickle the hem of my leggings before allowing them to creep slowly underneath the thin fabric. Toying with the delicate lace panties, I know my bedroom door is still open, but it only causes my heart to beat faster. I love the risk. The painful embarrassment of my dad catching me is an afterthought, because risk is always worth the reward.

The corner of my lip smirks, and with a hitched breath, my fingers slip under the last layer. Greeted by smooth familiarity, the anticipation builds and my nails trace mindless designs on bare skin. Goosebumps follow suit as I palm my pussy. My kitty immediately takes advantage, grinding slowly in return. Tingles electrify through my body. Slamming two fingers into my aching cunt, the frantic movements don't stop as I find the sensitive spot inside of me, adding to this feeling of euphoria and danger.

Toes flex and my legs vibrate. Each movement becomes rapid, more deliberate, to chase the release I so desperately am yearning for. I am in control now, and that's when it hits me like a ton of bricks. The lack of control over my life is the root problem. And this is the worst possible timing, dammit. I will not lose this orgasm. She is mine.

My clit tells me not all hope is lost, as we bring her back to life. Inserting a third finger, I continue riding myself while grinding against my nub. Maintaining a steady rhythm, it builds. Sweat beads on my face. Rapid heartbeats pound against my chest and in my ears. Panting, more of my body contracts. "Oh my god," I speak breathlessly.

The walls of my pussy contract around my fingers, which have been rubbing against that sweet spot perfectly. My clit throbs as my back arches. A loud moan escapes between my lips shamelessly as I come. My release coats me while riding the wave I wish never ends. If only an orgasm lasted over five seconds, so rude.

Not letting up, I do everything I can to extend its

stay inside of me, to no avail, the sweet tingling subsides, and my thighs clench for a final time before my body declares we are done.

Sliding my fingers out of my pussy, I hear the slick and smile. Bringing my hand out of my pants, I place all three fingers between my swollen lips and suck my cum off them. Lapping them with my tongue, the sweet and salty release is a welcomed treat to my taste buds.

Always eat pineapple, ladies. If you know, you know.

And sure, life advice from me right now is debatably not great. But I will take this fun fact to my grave, and will live by it until my last breath.

My tongue ensures it gets every drop off from around my fingers before sliding them out of my mouth. Allowing my eyes to remain closed, I relish this moment of relaxation that I have left. Multiple bodies mean I will be watching the moon set with the sunrise.

Hair sticks to my forehead. My body lays limp and relaxed on the ground with both hands resting on my chest, feeling the rapid beating of my heart.

A job well done. And now I am ready for a long night.

Before bringing movement back to my body, the most annoying voice invades my most sacred place.

"Next time, close your curtains. So help me, Harper. Nobody wants to see that." Merrick shouts from the tree he perches under, smoking his joint. Sadly, he has recently learned how to throw his voice around and tortures me regularly. I doubt he even saw anything. My house is miles away from where his boney ass is sitting. It was just a good guess. Fucker.

2. Harper

Skipping downstairs, headphones on, heavy metal serenades me, while still being very aware of my surroundings. Knuckles knock on the wall before rounding the corner. Shifting eyes wait with dread the longer he takes. Tight lips and flared nostrils.

Come on, not tonight, we don't have time for your shit tonight.

A heavy sigh follows. I'm irritated. Shaking my head, I raise my fist to bang on the wall once more. Before it can connect with the cool drywall, Dad's head peeks out, rolling his eyes at me. The audacity. Is he serious?

Relaxing my shoulders, muting my face from emotion, my response is a shrug. Tensions between us have been high as of late. The more I keep in, the less we address, and the further apart we grow. What more could he possibly expect? This family has some serious fucking issues.

I love my father. Adore him. He's an incredible man who has never pressured me and has allowed me to come into my own. But dark secrets torment souls. My silence has been viewed as an admission of guilt. Guilt by association. And some take every opportunity to remind me of it anytime I am in town, or at my best friend's house.

So, when I tell you the story, you won't believe it. But these eyes have seen things. Things they can never unsee. Understand, this isn't a child throwing a tantrum or being dramatic. The level of fuckup-ery is beyond anything Merrick could do or say. Which is monumental, in my humble opinion. For reference, he's the ghost with a tire-stained dick on his driveway. Who casually tells Hails how Joanie, her deceased grandmother, died as a bedtime story.

Now, think beyond that for what I am about to tell you. Are you ready? Comfortable?

Okay. Here we go.

And don't blame me or bill me for your therapy after this, because no one is paying for mine. You're on your own.

Mom's death was sudden.

Our grand staircase is made of beautifully aged antique ebony wood. Each scratch or dent is a memory, a moment in time that makes you smile. Black carpet trails down the center, going over each stair and lip. The purpose: I wouldn't slip and fall down them when I was a child. To give my tiny toes a grip when adventuring.

As I got older, the carpet stayed, blending into the house until that fateful day. Wear and tear thinned it out.

A body had just arrived and Mom had gotten changed and was on her way down to tend to them. Barefoot and shoeless, her big toe became trapped in a small, unnoticeable hole that had formed. Black on black, she would have never seen it.

Her body fell forward, a deafening scream echoing throughout the house. I was outside in the garden when I heard it. The air was warm, early summer, and the roses were getting ready to blossom. Mom's cry pricked my heart like a thorn. Acting on instinct and terror, my body raced to the house. Swinging the glass back door open, my eyes shifted around the empty kitchen and the house was suddenly silent.

Before I could move, shivers coated my body. And all the air inside of me rapidly vacated. It felt as if it was being sucked out of my soul and the moment it stopped, I fainted. Collapsing to the cool, white tiled floor.

Waking up, my long dark hair fanned out around me. I felt weak, pushing myself up onto my hands and knees, all my muscles trembling. The house was still quiet. Cautiously, once fully risen, my body moved of its own accord, taking me to the main entrance. Dad wasn't home. She died alone. Her neck at a ninety-degree angle.

I was sixteen.

I didn't see it happen. Dad was too distressed, and I wanted the truth. I needed it.

Still in shock, I asked the doctor, and told him no bullshit. He described what likely occurred based on evidence in the area and the story her dead body told. Scratch marks on the railing from her manicured nails told him she had tried to react, but the momentum, along with the surprise of the trip, prevented her from saving herself.

A larger dent, one I hadn't seen before, showed itself off on another step. He presumes that's where her neck snapped from the impact of her head against the hardwood.

This would be the first imperfection that caused grief and pain instead of smiles. And not the last.

Dad arrived home soon after I found her. His reaction is forever scarred into my heart. His eyes became vacant while his face paled. They were soulmates. That forever kind of love. He was on autopilot, not hearing the words I was speaking, only focusing on mom. His body moved him toward us, and he held her head in his lap until the EMTs finally arrived.

Being morticians, we both knew the cause of death: open cervical fracture in combination with a spinal cord injury, likely above the C5 vertebra as sharp bone had poked through the skin. A small pool of blood had formed.

Once they rotated her over, her chest was many shades of red and purple. Bruising indicating internal bleeding. Mom was gone. But I needed to understand it. And the doctor walked me through it, out loud, making it real. Seeing is believing, but hearing solidified the realness of it all.

This was the first time in all the years helping my parents with the deceased, this one, my mom, where I needed to know all the details. To be walked through it. Because a piece of my soul left me that day. An emptiness which has never been filled remains. And my dad, forever changed.

Dad decided almost immediately she was not being buried. He was keeping her. I held her hand for hours as she lay on the stainless-steel autopsy table, naked, vulnerable. I couldn't leave her alone like this. But I needed this time, just her and I, to begin processing that she was never coming back.

Once ready, I got up and started my work. First I straightened her neck back to normal and patched the punctures. Then, I washed her before Dad came down. It was peaceful, just us. Warm soapy water with a soft sponge cleaned all the dry blood off her beautiful skin. I lathered shampoo between my fingers and massaged her scalp, followed by conditioner. Then combed her hair gently, letting her natural wave appear as it dried. Red polish coated her nails.

I had to remove her jewelry. Her yellow gold jewelry sits on a tray now, cold and alone. They will be reunited with Mom soon enough, their forever home.

Peacefully Mom sleeps, eyes closed, lips slightly parted. My eyes watch her chest, delusionally. Not blinking, I wait for it to rise, just once. That's all we need, and then she will be back to us. Please, Mom, *please*.

I'm not sure how long I sat with her after. Minutes, which may have turned into hours. I lost track of time as my focus was purely her.

Dad's footsteps were slow and heavy coming down to the basement. He insisted on embalming her. And once he's done I would cover her bruises with makeup and apply Mom's favorite lipstick; the shade always reminds me of dark dried blood in a morbidly beautiful way.

Fitting, I suppose.

Two hours is all it took to embalm her. Dad injected Mom with ten liters of solution. The maximum a body could handle, to ensure the highest chance of perfect preservation. I followed, doing her makeup and dressing her in beautiful florals. It reminded me of her garden. Mom's pride and joy after myself and dad. That's when Dad informed me he was having a chamber built, a temperature-controlled glass enclosure.

Our refrigerator can keep a cadaver preserved for one to three weeks, tops. It's not the long-term solution my dad needed, though. The chamber would have to maintain a below-freezing temperature to be worth his efforts. Even if I didn't agree, I supported his right to have this choice.

Once I slid her thin gold band back onto her ring finger, I kissed her hand, said my silent goodbyes, and left them alone.

I know this shit is heavy. But you have to understand the past to fully comprehend the present. And we haven't even hit the part that requires several sessions of therapy. Because to me and my family, this is normal. Our lives are dedicated to the nonliving. To those who no longer can tell a story through their voice, but only through clues left behind on and within their bodies. They are my passion. And has been my family's passion for centuries.

This is my legend, my legacy, and my responsibility.

And what I am about to share with you now taints that legacy. And perhaps I am no longer proud to carry it on. But those words shall never be spoken out loud. No one will ever suspect the heavy burden placed upon me that fateful day. They will strictly see what I want them to.

Mom stayed in the refrigerator unit for a week before Dad's glass chamber arrived, compliments of Merrick's now drug dealer. Apparently, he is also good at science and building shit. Dad had him include brown leather straps to keep Mom standing upright.

And at first, once I saw her there, standing in our basement, disgust immediately came to mind. Not at her but at his concept, and I slightly freaked out. Then, as time passed, I didn't mind it. I actually thought it was nice.

To come downstairs and talk to her whenever I wanted was my favorite pastime. Endless hours of gossip and rambling while preparing bodies was a welcome change to my usual routine. I didn't feel alone. And it made the grieving process easier, I think. Or perhaps it prolonged it?

This is where therapy would come in handy.

If Dad had just buried her, I could go visit her in the cemetery once settled, and Mom could speak back to me. We could have conversations. Stay up all night under the stars, laughing. Instead, this was my new normal; I accepted it.

Months had passed, the town had begun to talk, and rumors circulated. None of which I paid any attention to. I knew my dad, but they didn't.

That's when resentment built, and there was nothing I could do to stop it. All I could do was mask the impact our new life had upon me. And as a teenager, shit is already really hard.

One morning, just as I was about to go into our back garden, I heard a commotion coming from the basement. To my knowledge, I was home alone. With a racing heart, I rushed into the kitchen and took a knife swiftly out of the wooden butcher's block. Tiptoeing around the island, my body led me to the basement door.

Pressing an ear to the thick wood barrier, silence greeted me. Maybe the intruder heard me. Gently, my fingers grasped the cool iron knob, turning it until the latch clicked. Hinges creaked upon opening. A loud grunt followed. Concern and confusion caused my brow to furrow. Hushed steps took me down. The knife handle was still in my hand. Adrenaline took over. And before I know it, I was standing in the open doorway, coming face to face... or back, with the intruder.

Except they weren't an intruder.

It felt like millions of tiny bugs were crawling over my body. I wanted to escape but couldn't move. Dad was almost naked. His saggy ass greeted me, followed by more heavy grunting. His heels rose as his calves flexed, thrusting. I think I may have vomited. The glass door to Mom's chamber was open. And the one place I truly enjoyed been taken away from me.

I love him, but I also hate him so fucking much.

Where seeing is believing, I can now confirm the rumors are true. And no, I don't know if his dick has frostbite or if her frozen cunt warms up for him during it.

And by defiling my mom, he has ruined everything.

The knife fell from my fingers. Rattling against the white square titles. He was startled. Then stopped. But he didn't turn around to face me. Instead, Dad lowered himself to his feet and bent down to the pile of clothes around him. Mom's dress, tucked up and over her breasts, was exposing her. Cum runs down Mom's thighs. And he couldn't even fucking face me.

Coward.

3. HARPER

Dad has never acknowledged it.
But he knows I know. He knows the town talks.

And *him* fucking my dead mother's body became our new normal. The headphones and knocking before entering is routine. Less precautions are taken when I know with no doubt he isn't down there. Resentment existed for years. And in the pit of my stomach, a grudge remains, but it has become less prominent in my life. Anger surged through my veins at the sight of Dad, or his scent. It was unbearable, and I finally allowed myself to let go of the hate. But there is always one thing I will always believe: it will not waver. Selfishness tainted a quiet sanctuary filled with love and passion, caretaking and ritualistic energies.

It was around the same time I let go that I found solace in the graveyard.

I had always explored. Nature is my home away from home. Our property is significantly larger than most in Port Canyon. I acknowledge I have grown up privileged and blessed, so if you want to feel bad for me, you may, but you don't need to cry for me. A little emotional scarring has gone a long way with me.

A long, lonely night led me outside mid-spring. I couldn't sleep. The moon shined bright upon me as I maneuvered the paths in my yard. From the corner of my eye, I glimpsed at the tall, dark iron fence surrounding Joanie Knight's property, the grave keeper. The old woman was a cunt. Try to find a person to dispute it, I dare you. It won't happen. And the was *is intentional, because she's dead now. My bestie killed her, and I had the honor to witness such greatness in person.*

But when the bitch was alive, she gave 'trespassers will be prosecuted' vibes. No one dared to even attempt to enter the property uninvited. Until I did. This was during the 'no fucks to give' phase of my grieving. And it was alarmingly easy to get onto her property, which conveniently is located across the street from me. The gap between the bars was wider than I am, so I simply slipped on through. No super stealth mission required until I hit the backyard.

The large floor-to-ceiling glass windows at the back of the house had my heart racing. In Converse sneakers, baggy blue jeans, and a black tee, I stuck close to the lush green hedges and snuck around the large angel statue positioned in the middle of the yard. With only the moonlight aiding me, I hoped I was going the right way. And that Joanie wouldn't catch me. Too afraid to look toward the windows, I continued on until I came across an arch in the hedges accompanied by a small iron gate. Shaking fingers reached out before me. Finding the latch, a chill washed over me. A loud squeak echoed when I pushed the gate open. My brows scrunched in worry. Instead of freezing, I only moved quicker. The bitch is old. I could outrun her.

Rushing through the arch, I swung the gate hard, closing it behind me. My feet padded down the path. Large branches swayed with the breeze overtop of me. The rustling of long grass joined in. Fresh fragrance of wildflowers filled my nose. And calmness washed over me. My new safe space found.

Slowing my pace, shadows of large gravestones loomed over me. And another large angel statue greeted me. I'll have to come back in daylight to get a better look at them. This entire place fascinates me. The energy I expected to be spooky and uneasy is oddly comforting and warm.

That first night, I explored until the sun peaked. A mausoleum overrun by vines, aged headstones which had crumbled, and a couple fresher graves were all I could explore, but it took hours. The place has to be acres upon acres. I'd go back the following night, and the one after that. Until I became brave and risked the daylight.

Never caught once, and I am proud of that. If I heard Joanie approaching with her heavy steps, I would hide in the thick forest until the coast was clear. There was one time when I was otherwise distracted, lost in a book resting against a giant tree. I wasn't paying attention. And Darla appeared before me, out of thin air, and frantically whispered, "Girl, go. She's nearly here!"

I knew the role of the grave keeper was to help those transition over. But I had never seen a ghost before. They stayed in the graveyard. Darla was my first one, and she was helping me, looking out for me. It surprised me and completely caught me off guard. With a racing heart, I closed my book and Darla disappeared as quickly as she arrived. I didn't have time to go to the lush foliage. Joanie dry heaving, which never made sense because Port Canyon had in a moist climate, told me she was seconds away from spotting me.

I hopped over a few gravestones before finding one tall enough to offer me cover. Watching the sun in the sky helped me gage the time. It was primarily quiet until

Joanie started her usual bitching. "You ungrateful cowards. I care for you. Go out of my way each day to help you. And you don't even show yourselves." And this wasn't the first time I had heard her barking at the spirits. And it hurt my soul for them. They don't deserve her hostility and self-importance.

Then realization washed over me. Darla, who at the time I didn't know as Darla, showed herself to me. She trusted me enough to do so. She knows how unbearable Joanie is and wanted to save me from such ugliness. I promised myself that day to never take them for granted. The process would be slow, but I would do my best to show them the love and respect they deserved in the afterlife.

It also occurred to me my dad may have saved Mom from an afterlife of misery.

Closing off the last stitch over the young man's thick brow, I put the thread and needle down and clean the area with damp gauze. I've changed his clothes already, so he is in similar jeans and a long-sleeve Henley shirt. His shoes remain the same. Shaggy brown hair washed and drying into soft curls. He looks young, maybe freshly eighteen?

His family will miss him, mourn him, and slowly move on, but never forget him. The car will be found. They will know the town has him now and that we will take great care of him. Perhaps not this October, but next, they will come to see him and he will see them. But only when he is ready. Because transitioning is hard, and strange, and Fallon never rushes the process. She's the most caring and compassionate grave keeper. I am forever grateful for the day she killed Joanie. The spirits deserved better, and now have it.

These bodies won't be embalmed, nor will the bruising be covered with makeup. Another male and one female lay still before me.

We rarely use embalming fluid when transferring bodies to the graveyard. But we have the supplies should they ever be requested. Hence my mother's interesting situation. We added some to Joanie to ensure she never returned. We want that miserable old spirit glued inside of her, with no chance of escaping.

And if you have read Merrick's chaotic memoir, *Ghost Dick*, you would know why we rarely do the full processing on bodies in town. I fully acknowledge it's Fallon's story, but the guy has an ego. My bestie doesn't.

Fuck, please don't tell him I even recited such words. Recommending his memoir, God, I want to vomit. He drives me mental. And I know he gets off on it, which makes my stomach turn further at the thought. But it seems to be his only hobby, fucking with people. After each successful sarcastic remark, I bet he looks at Fallon, all proud of himself. "Come on. I just insulted your friend and made her mildly uncomfortable. Let me slam my cock inside of you."

I never take it personally. He was born an asshole. He can't help it. But sometimes it stings. I am human, after all.

Low blow, I know. But I don't care.

Enough reminiscing. You have the important bits, which are key to why I am now on a bridge, or was, until my body flew through the air and landed on damp grass on the side of the riverbank.

So, let's recap. My mom died, and I found her. Dad started fucking her dead body after I prepared her, and continues to do so. Perhaps later tonight, even. Merrick, who is annoying but not a major player in this equation, keeps my bestie occupied a lot and pregnant with his dick. I love her babies. And I love her, endlessly. But major FOMO is happening in my brain and I can't help it. I am lonely, and feeling left behind. What is my purpose beyond all of this?

It's been thirty minutes, and we found the root cause of this lost and low moment in life, all without a therapist. We saved three hundred dollars. And instead of talking to one stranger, I talked to all of you. Basically, making us friends now. Dare I say potential bestie status?

You're welcome. Happy to have you.

"Sweetie, go rest. You look exhausted. I'll let Fallon know they are ready, and bring the souls over in the van," my dad generously volunteers, looking as tired as I am.

Nodding, I don't object. While I have treated our souls with respect and care, my mind is roaming elsewhere. Lost in thought. Thinking of the past and not living in the present.

Rising from my black swivel stool, I toe my shoes off, not wanting to contaminate the house with blood and other fluids that had dripped on them. Removing the surgical gloves, I toss them in the biohazard bin along with the gown. Without looking back, I wish Dad a sleepy farewell. "Night, Dad. Love you."

His warm voice follows, "Love you, too."

4. Harper

Clearing my head, I escape the confines of my compounds.

To be clear, I didn't know I would end up at the bridge until I did. Mindlessly, my body led me through our majestic town full of old English Victorian architecture and history. Cobblestones under my shoes with the large clock tower in the center of town comfort me. Passion for Port Canyon runs rampant through my veins. It's a mind and body connection. Breathing in the familiar cool, damp air through my nose and into my lungs brings a smile to my stoic face. Brushing fingertips against the rigid walls of the buildings, I am comforted.

This is my home.

Leaving the town center, the well-lit walkway

becomes more dim. Lampposts spread farther apart and my shadow disappears behind me. A chill ripples over my bare arms. Not thinking, I didn't grab a jacket before leaving. Adding a skip to my step, my long hair in its high ponytail sways while passing empty fields.

Homes in Port Canyon sit on large properties, secluded from nosey neighbors, like me.

Since breaching Joanie's perimeters like a super spy agent, no one's yards were safe from me any longer. Merrick's drug dealer was my second mission. From the outside, you would never know he had a grow-op. But like Joanie's, once you got into the backyard, the mystery revealed itself. And for Mr. Drug Dealer, his yard presented me with what acres of weed plants looked like.

I've never tempted fate with marijuana. The smell is pungent and I imagine I would be the paranoid type on it. The trip would trip me and by the end, I would be even more confused than I was at the beginning. And I bet you got confused reading that, so do you see what I mean? Even at the thought, my mind can't handle it.

But I bring this up because we are about to pass his house. No gates protect it, but cameras and infrared sensors do. It gave me more of a challenge and I fucking loved it.

Looking over, the large brownstone manor has lights lining the long drive. An upstairs light is on, two shadows show themselves through the white curtains, and I am tempted to stop and watch further. Lips connect, arms wrap around one another, and the bodies sway. Briefly they part, one pushes the other, and they fall backward as the one standing follows.

Rude!

Rolling my eyes in a huff of disappointment, my feet continue our journey. And that's when I hear the calming river flowing.

The infamous bridge nears. And my feet take me there.

A misty fog forms before me the closer I get. The tall mountain peaks fade and a single light attempts to shine through it on the opposite side. Revealing where the bridge meets land once more. I stop at the edge of town. Closing my now heavy eyes, my ears absorb the beauty of the rushing river hitting the banks and crashing against the rocks.

Rustling branches from wildlife wandering. Taking a deep breath, my mind rests, the loud thoughts stop. Instinct mixed with impulse takes over and my body moves forward.

My heart pounds against my chest. Footsteps echo with each step. I wasn't alive when it happened, but

Dad kept the articles from the day Merrick drove himself off the bridge. Opening my eyes, I come to an abrupt stop. Glancing down, my feet stand on top of the same skid marks left behind from that day.

The marks are not from him changing his mind. But from the sharp turn he made, directing his vehicle toward the railing. Merrick's back tires skidded across the flat top of the bridge before pushing through the metal barrier and plummeting below.

Like his father, who passed prior to Merrick, he remained hidden for decades. But unlike his father, he reappeared when Fallon arrived. She made him curious and he made us mental. But eventually, he won her over, and later he showed his strength as her partner, supporting her as she killed his mother. It's so incredibly romantic.

But I will deny admitting any of this. His pestering will only increase and he will not win this war.

Back to the bridge. It's around this time I wail into the night and throw my arms out wide when the silence of nature is interrupted. The squeaks of the tires accompany the loud rumble of a car engine. Tires grip the tarmac as the car maneuvers the windy roads through the mountain range. And the thoughts of why Merrick ended it all encourage my mind to turn back and reflect upon my own life.

It's wildly depressing.

My thoughts move to the car driver and passengers. The town will reject them and we will have more bodies to prepare. And as you also know, I whispered sadly into the night sky, my breath dancing before my eyes before disappearing, "I love you, I'm sorry," in hopes my dad would hear it.

Then, just as the car approaches, its horn honks, followed by loud hooting and hollering. I had decided my fate would be this. Therefore, I do not move. The roaring engine rumbles. Vibrations riddle me as the car drives onto the bridge. Adrenaline courses through me, like I am playing a game of chicken, knowing neither of us will move.

Is this what freedom tastes like?

My brain expects the impact to occur within seconds. I count down in my head, three, two... one.

One comes, and I'm hit from the side. The impact knocks the wind out of me and my feet fly off the ground. My body feels ice cold as it moves through the air. My mind wonders, is this what it's like to die? Everything moving in slow motion so you can absorb it all before it ends? At least it doesn't hurt.

And as that thought leaves me, my body collides with the hard ground. Damp grass sticks to my cheek and my head bounces, giving me whiplash. Reaching up, the back of my hand wipes my hair off my face. Looking up, I attempt to get my bearings, but I am stunned speechless. Everything just got a million times more complicated.

Strong hands continue to grip me, and shivers tingle up my spine.

My savior's embrace is cool to the touch. Catching me off guard as I place my hands on his bulging biceps. I then realize my body is reacting before my concussed brain. Taken aback, I quickly release him, frantically pushing myself backward on the damp ground. His hands stay on my waist. And he remains kneeling before me.

The guy has long arms. He must be tall.

Never looking away, I take in the person before me. His hair is voluminous. Silky long waves hang just below his chin. Piercing blue eyes with dark, long lashes captivate me. And his manly but groomed short beard decorates his strong jawline. Fuck, why do men always have the best lashes and apparently hair now too?

Focusing back on my mystery man, worry lines embed themselves into his forehead. If I were to guess his age, I would think mid-to-late forties. The vein in his neck is bulging. And it appears as if I have perhaps angered him. How exciting! If I can't die by a random game of chicken, who is also on a suicide mission, perhaps my savior turned serial killer is my fate. But for the record, I do not know if that is his occupation, yet. Let us not lose hope!

Testing the waters, I cough an attitude. "No one asked you to save me. Can you kindly remove your strong manly hands from my hips?" I pester, knowing it will only provoke him. But it's part of my charm.

He doesn't respond. Glaring back at him, my eyes travel frantically up and down his fit body. Wearing a black tee and matching black jeans and combat boots. No fucking way.

It's Gabriel Knight.

5. Gabriel

Please allow me to start by apologizing for my son. Merrick has always been his own spirit. Insert dad joke here.

Peering down at the frightened girl before me, her face freezes. She's in shock. It's like she has just seen a ghost. Oh, it's because she has.

Okay, last dad joke, I promise. For now...

Harper Hayes. Eyes that hypnotize.

They aren't a classic bright blue. No, they are darker, mysterious, and curious. They are a contrast to her delicate pale skin, long dark hair, and lashes. I'd say they are more of a slate blue, pulling me in further until I get lost and make her my home.

My fingers grip her waist, not wanting to let go. I

can't. What if she tries *it* again? I'm not losing the only light in my life. The one I watch over and protect.

Harper Hayes has given purpose in to an afterlife which hasn't had one for decades.

Still frightened, she tries to pull back and, reluctantly, I let go.

Balancing back on my heels, I tilt my head, awaiting her next move. A piece of long hair falls over my forehead. Raking my fingers through the locks, I push it out of the way. In return, Harper watches curiously. The moon bounces off one of my gold rings. Her eye glints, and I smile.

I thought she was going to move.

"Why didn't you move?"

My outburst catches me by surprise. These are the first words I have verbalized since I passed.

Murdered. I was murdered.

Let's tell it like it is, shall we? I'm not here to sugarcoat anything. Death was a peaceful passing. Because how Joanie murdered me was painless. The cunt did one thing right. But I won't thank her. Absolutely not. Singing praises for Joanie is a tune I do not recognize.

But that's a story for another day. Because right now, Harper needs us.

Watching her intently, Harper's head shakes in

disbelief. I nod curtly, encouraging her to answer my question. I crave understanding.

"Because I felt something new. It was exhilarating. I don't actually want to die. But I also don't enjoy being me, sometimes, I suppose."

Her perfectly pink lips close for only a moment. "I knew what their fate would be. What they would become. And how I would prepare them. But for the first time in my life, I didn't know what would happen to me. I didn't need to be Harper. No one relied on me. I didn't need to mask deep family-rooted trauma, and it felt incredible." Gazing down, her hands play with the long grass mindlessly. Her eyes stare off into the distance as she gets lost inside her head.

"Why did you do it?"

Her question catches me off guard.

The answer is simple. "You deserve to live."

Tears well in her beautiful eyes, and my heart aches at the sight of her pain.

"Let me save you."

The words slip out, and I instantly regret it. Fuck, what is wrong with me? I'm mortified. Not because I don't mean it, I do. But because it's way too fucking soon. Word vomit. That's me. And tonight, I will spiral briefly, overanalyzing how those four words will have impacted everything moving forward.

"I don't even know you." Harper looks absolutely repulsed. Her face contorts, body closes up, bringing her knees into her chest as she wraps her arms around them.

But I know her.

Having always stayed in the farthest corner of the graveyard, I kept my distance from everyone and everything. Resentment was the likelihood. Merrick did the same thing, but hid in plain sight. His hate guided him until *she* showed up.

Word traveled fast. Fallon was here and change was imminent, thanks to a perky girl named Harper Hayes. She pushed Fallon to ask questions and find answers. She is courageous, brave, and the sole reason everything changed for the better in Port Canyon.

The night of the ceremony, I remained hidden, watching from the front row alongside both my sons, Merrick and Mark.

And instead of eavesdropping on tales from other spirits, I finally saw *her*. Harper.

Immediate infatuation. Obsession.

Gravity pulled me toward her, and I allowed it. She stood in support of her best friend. Pride radiated from her and my dick was instantly hard. Nothing is sexier than a confident woman, and with those eyes, I was done for. She had me hooked and didn't even know it.

Her dad stood next to her.

Something I had given no thought to until Merrick made a snide remark in passing. Then I had to see it, to believe. For research purposes only. Of course.

Her father, Doug Hayes, is one sick yet kinky fucker. Holds no shame or remorse and he actually likes how his dick feels inside of his dead wife. Truly fascinating. I once heard him whispering, *"I will feel you warm again. I've been practicing."*

He spends hours masturbating.

That man must be experiencing the early onset of carpel tunnel. His goal is to fuck her long enough for her pussy to defrost around him. To feel her slick walls clamp around his cock, milking him until his hairy old man balls are wrung dry.

She'll never come on his dick again.

It's an effort wasted, with serious long-term repercussions.

And yes, I have watched. Dick remained soft; I wasn't completely creepy about it, apparently.

Can't a man be curious? Several times?

But back to Harper. Who is shivering before me. Goosebumps decorate her exposed skin. The adrenaline has worn off, realization of the current situation sets in, and I hope she lets me save her.

6. Harper

His voice soothes the soul and moistens my panties.

Blinking rapidly, I can't believe it. Am I hallucinating?

I've seen photos around the Knight estate. And when Mom would tell me tales as a kid. She would bring out her photo album to help me visualize every story. To learn every legend and legacy. Every Polaroid told me another thousand words she may have missed. And his face was in many of those stories.

It's Gabriel fucking Knight.

Disbelief and shock, I, out of nowhere, speak words. Audible, loud, inner-thoughts words. It's completely unexpected for both of us. "Are you a predator?"

The question is valid. He's really fucking old. But Jesus, I am never this blunt and abrasive.

Gabriel's brows rise, eyes widen, exposing deep wrinkles on his forehead.

The man, or ghost, is rightfully taken aback and quite possibly insulted. But that doesn't bother me because my question is the most important question of them all. No one has seen him since he died, or so my mom told me.

Why now? Why me? And how long has he been watching? How exposed have I been to this man without my knowledge, physically and emotionally?

This is all predator behavior. And it's making my panties wet in the worst way. I've never had a stalker before. I'm almost flattered. Fear is the dominant one of this battle, my horniness is being forced to take a back seat.

Freshwater crashes against the banks, helping fill the silence surrounding us after my abrupt question. Glancing around, I finally get my bearings. Gabriel has brought us a few miles down the river, away from the attention of the bridge and impending car crash. Which, for clarity, would have happened with or without me. None of that situation is my fault.

A light mist falls over us. Or through him? But definitely on me.

Goosebumps become more prominent on my exposed skin. Reaching out, the bed of his cool thumb touches my skin, tracing circles in comfort. My breath hitches. His lips part. And ever so seriously, Gabriel speaks. "I am not a predator, Harper."

Narrowing my eyes suspiciously, I am fully aware this is a classic predator response. He is attempting to gaslight me, and it won't work. But I will play along if it gets me out of here and home to a warm bath.

Peering up wide-eyed, Gabriel is still crouched down and worry riddles his face.

"Okay." And that one simple word immediately changes his demeanor. Shoulders relax, the mindless circles turn into figure eights, and his head falls with his chin resting on his chest.

Reaching forward, my fingers rake through his soft, flowy locks. He shivers from the intrusion but doesn't stop me. Instead, I stop myself, the realization of my movements hitting me, and I pull back immediately. Moving myself farther away from Gabriel, instant regret follows. What is wrong with me?

"I don't need to be saved," I blurt out.

Pain enters his expression, his eyes close, head nodding, as he understands my words. Which I find relief in, because I mean them.

"Take me home. Now!"

My tone is demanding, but necessary. It would appear living on the edge of danger is something I now crave and I cannot nearly cave to it twice in one night. Hurt washes over his face next, the sadness in his eyes gives it away, followed by a defeated nod of the head.

Without further hesitation, Gabriel's moving before I can even register it. Arms scoop me up, sending another chilling reaction down my spine and to my ovaries. He holds me close against his chest, and naturally I nestle in looking for warmth which cannot be found.

He's a ghost.

Mist continues to fall, each breath becoming more visible as my body shakes. Quiet words are whispered. "You will not have the same tragic ending as my son."

My beating heart breaks into two halves for this man. The thought never occurred to me. But this isn't the same. Merrick and I aren't the same. We have had two different journeys, his were miles far more unbearable than mine. I love my family, my life, this town, and my friends. My parents have always filled my life knowing what to expect at the end of the rainbow. With minor hiccups, like having to mask the hurt I feel when people bring up my dad. Or escaping and finding joy in said escape in the cemetery. The bubbly personality I keep up is the biggest mask of all. But I am not suicidal. I get fed up, absolutely exhausted by it all. Ultimately, I think it's because I just want to feel life, the unexpected experiences of life. The unknown. Will the car break?

Oh, my word, am I a thrill seeker?

This has really been a tremendous evening of self-reflection. Good job, team!

Leaning into Gabriel, my racing mind settles, and it is now my turn to comfort him. He has been unliving with this sadness for decades and is perhaps trying to make up for it.

But please note: I am not a damsel in distress. Harper fucking Hayes doesn't need saving. No, you stop that. He did not save me from a possible impending death moments ago. I don't care how it may be perceived currently, because it didn't happen. The man is a predator.

Gabriel moves quickly, taking us around the perimeter of town to avoid being seen. It only takes one chatty neighbor to spot us and all of Port Canyon will know by sunrise, which is due anytime now.

Trees move swiftly past us, the scent of fresh rain fills my nose, and nausea occupies my stomach. This is a ride I need to get off of soon before my dinner trails behind us. Tiny burps continue and panic strikes. What if it smells? Can ghosts smell? This is mortifying.

Distracted, Gabriel takes us higher off the ground. Causing my body to tense in his hold. Words of comfort follow. "We just went over your fence." I don't respond.

Our movement slows. Each passing hedge and shrub become less blurred in my vision. Then both his feet plant themselves firmly on the green grass. Gingerly, Gabriel places me down, holding my waist as the dizzy spell evaporates. Giving my head a shake, a deep chuckle sneaks out. My head spins, eyes glare as I shoo his hands off me. "What?" I feel insulted. He could have waited until after. To openly laugh at me after allegedly wanting to save me is rude.

Waving his hand off, the surrounding garden lights allow me to see him better. Light reflects off a couple gold rings decorating his strong manly hands, accompanied by a matching gold watch. Focusing on it, I see it ticks no more.

"My time of death." He noticed. How morbid. I kind of like it.

Taking him in fully, for the first time I notice Gabriel is taller than Merrick, but he has a similar fashion sense with the boots and tight jeans. I see both his boys in him. They have his eyes, sculpted jawline, and unconventional reappearing act. Like Merrick, Gabriel hadn't been seen since his death, until tonight, to my knowledge. But Mark, who seems to share the same compassionate gene, reappeared instantly once he was brought to the graveyard. Interesting. All so similar yet so very opposite. I am finding myself deeply invested the longer I stand here, in the misting rain, staring at him.

Curious eyes look back at me. "You are the most peculiar girl," Gabriel murmurs to himself. As if his mouth spoke words only meant for his head.

I am not one easily offended; I tolerate my bestie's baby daddy daily. So I own that shit. "Fuckin' right, I am." I smirk back sarcastically.

Orange and beautiful reds dance across the surrounding ground. Willow trees, wildflowers, and the calming stream fill the void of words. Birds sing, waking from a slumber, while owls close their heavy eyelids, seeking rest.

The misting rain starts to lift, allowing the rising sun to further peek through morning clouds as it climbs over the mountains.

For the town has taken another soul or two, the town weeps for the lost souls, but welcomes them home.

Long lashes bat against pale white cheeks. Gabriel's focus lingers on me.

Okay, so it's now painfully obvious I haven't had a dick in some time. Because the moment his hand rises to stroke his trimmed beard, it does things to me. My nipples harden more intensely under my wet shirt. His forearm flexes. Can he sense it?

Taking one step forward, I retreat one step back. Anxiety follows as the events of this evening rumble in my head. And I will continue to overanalyze them for days to come. Followed by beating myself up over the stupidity of it all and hiding in embarrassment, even if nobody technically saw me or knew.

But I am now a thrill seeker. It's the one takeaway from the chaos I created this evening. Oh, and Gabriel holds deep regret. I also have several questions about his death. I hope he didn't think we were candy-glazing over that bomb. Because we most definitely did not.

I think Mom would be proud of me. I overcame a lot this evening to find myself while still loving the path I am meant to take.

Spinning around on my toes, waving a single hand loosely around in the air, Gabriel speaks first.

"Where are you going?" His deep and delicious voice vibrates off me.

Shaking my head, "Be gone with you, predator," I

shout into the sky, not worrying about if my voice will carry. A faint chuckle follows. Clenching my thighs tight while walking through the brush toward home, it would appear I am suddenly very horny once more.

GABRIEL

Watching her walk away is a sight I want to burn into my memory. Her sassy hips sway as she owns this fucking yard. I have waited my entire death for you, Harper Hayes. And if you desire a predator, then I shall be your predator. Happily. As I have already been watching you for many moons.

7. Harper

"My dad and Darla are banging."

The entire sentence is not one I ever expected to hear from my best friend.

"Excuse me while I pick my jaw off the ground." My comment sends her cackling. "No, you can't laugh like this. You'll end up going into early labor." But my concern is apparently hilarious because tears follow. I'm positive she would be on the ground kicking her Converse-clad feet, if it wasn't impossible for her to get up after.

Gasping, I hope the answer to my question is no. "Wait! Does Merrick know?"

"That's the best part. He has no idea."

This is the best day ever. Thank you, holy ghost, for making all my dreams come true. The fun we will have with this and all the while, he is completely fucking oblivious. I don't know what I have done to deserve such a gift, but thank you. I swear I could nearly cry with excitement.

Sitting on the floor in Fallon's library, my bum wiggles giddily as my toes tap the hardwood. I have so many questions like, "How did you find out?"

Merrick is out in the graveyard with Hails and that nasty naughty girl, Darla. So Fallon and I are free to gossip until our heart's desire, or until it's dinnertime.

Her cheeks turn red, eyelashes fluttering as she bites her lip.

"No, you are not having this baby yet. You are just as nasty as Darla. No getting off on sexy time memories!" I playfully shout, breaking Fallon from her sexy-eyes trance.

She giggles in response. "I've been painfully horny with this pregnancy. I need it day and night. The way he hits it then rotates inside of me makes my body tingle all over." Her eyes hood and I could vomit at any moment if this doesn't get to Darla and Mark soon. "Apparently, the other night, I was moaning in my sleep, clenching my thighs tight and rocking my hips. And as you know, Merrick loves fucking me filthy in my sleep."

An authentic gag follows as she continues. "I came

so hard it woke me up. My legs were raised sky high. My pajama shorts were torn off me. Merricks cock hitting my cervix. You would think he was curved, but he isn't. My baby daddy is just that incredible." An audible burp from me follows her vile declaration.

"After he came on my pussy instead of inside, because he loves painting me with his cum, I needed to tidy up, because nobody wants a yeast infection. Merrick went to smoke a joint under his tree. That was the same night he learned how to throw his voice, actually. Anyhow, after handling my business, I went downstairs for water, because hydration is important. As soon as I hit the stairs, I heard the grunts. And because of my horny pregnant state, I knew immediately what those grunts meant. Sex."

Rubbing my hands together, finally, we are getting to the good part.

"Tiptoeing down each step, I strategically avoided the spots which creak before hitting the ground floor. In my fuzzy socks, I slide along the floor, toward the formal dining room. That's when I heard a voice and froze. *'you are so fucking tight, my sexy little bitch.'*... It was my dad!"

We both scream at the same time. This is wild. But I need to know more. "Okay. Then what? You didn't stay and watch, did you? It's your dad!"

Fallon's face contorts, she is visibly disgusted at the thought of watching, yet she didn't mind listening. This girl is next level with this baby.

"I did not. But I took a peek. I noticed him and Darla getting close after my ceremony. But neither of them said anything, so I played along as if nothing was happening. But the moment I peered around the corner through the kitchen entrance, I saw it with my own two eyes. Dad had Darla bent over the kitchen island, ramming himself into her from behind. Thankfully, his head was thrown back and her forehead was against the granite top. And I wanted to squeal with excitement, but couldn't. So, I scurried back upstairs and into the bathroom and did the happiest of dances before drinking some water from the tap."

I hold my hands up, needing more information. "Did they ever find out you saw them?" With wide eyes, Fallon nods, smiling. "Yes. I told Darla during one of our graveyard chats the other day. I couldn't keep it in, it's all just so exciting. Do you know how long it's been since she's had dick? Like, a hundred years. Am I absolutely grossed out that I heard and saw my dad having sex? Yes, absolutely. But I don't think about that part. I think about Darla finally getting the D."

I have to give it to my friend. She is a better person than me, because I have seen my dad sexing, and it is forever burnt into my memory. Every time I close my eyes, it flashes before me like a bad porno before falling asleep.

"Merrick is going to die when he finds out his brother is fucking her. I can't wait to see his reaction. Because I know how overly dramatic it will be." She claps her hands frantically together at the thought and I must admit, that part is going to be fucking epic.

Then, if he ever finds out Daddy is back, he may have a stroke. Oh my god, can ghosts have strokes? Heart attacks? No, it can't be possible. His tantrum will be one from the history books, and I will happily add it to the Knight section. *The Ghost Who Shit Himself* could be the title. Then I think back to the other night, with Gabriel, and something drops into the pit of my stomach. There is something about that man I can't stop thinking about.

Clearing her throat, Fallon interrupts my thoughts. "Okay, dreamy eyes, what is going on inside that pretty head of yours?"

Busted. *Shit.*

Shaking my head, I wave her off. "Nothing. Well, okay. I am picturing it. Your dad and Darla. That shit is hot, Fallon. Quality spank bank material, as they say." Please buy it. I am not ready to share my secrets yet. Especially since I don't know what it all means yet.

I haven't seen him since his 'I need to save you' bullshit. Typical male, all talk and no action. But fuck, I would kill to feel his soft brown locks between my fingers one last time. The man is sexy. And my pussy is aching. Down, girl, it's never going to happen.

Fallon squeals at my false admission. "Ew. Stop. That's my dad! Harper Hayes, you are just as nasty as Darla. I swear."

I raise my hand at her playful acquisition and throw a cheeky wink. "Guilty as charged."

"Harp-Harp!" a familiar toddler excitedly calls out from the back of the house.

Fallon calls out to her. "In here, sweet girl." Cute giggles and a brooding ghost join us. Hail's eyes are wide and her body vibrates in excitement.

"Did you know? I learned this from Nan-Nan Darla. Did you know Daddy should be arrested?!"

Merrick rolls his eyes, waving the fun fact off. "Baby, I own this place, no one is arresting me."

Hands on her hips, Hails turns to her dad and stomps her tiny foot. "Mommy runs this joint. Don't you ever forget that." And that sends me off into a fit of hysterical laughter. Fallon covers her mouth, waiting to see how this will end.

"Mommy doesn't like joints, but she loves Daddy's sausage in her donut." If Fallon could get up on her own, I know she would be on her feet scolding her baby daddy. Instead, she swats at his legs. "Mommy won't like that either if Daddy keeps talking out loud."

Hails jumps in quicker than a rabbit. "Like the donut daddy made on the driveway?"

Merrick winks, before glancing toward me, and feeds his daughter's inquiring mind, proudly. "Yes. Just like that!" Then skipping all the pleasantries, he greets me. "Harper."

I nod and formally state his name. "Merrick." Pushing myself up off the ground, I follow that with a bow. Hails finds it funny and follows my lead. Could this day get any better?

"Good sir, I am happy you could return before nightfall. But I am afraid you interrupted m'lady Hails. Please go on, tell us why Daddy should be arrested."

Hails stands tall, tiny finger in the air now. "Because swearing in front of corpses is illegal! And Daddy swears all the fucking time in the graveyard, Darla says." I burst out laughing once more. Fallon can't help herself and joins in while holding her bouncing belly.

Bending down, I scratch Hails head, and whisper, "Never change, baby girl."

Looking up to me with those beautiful doe eyes,

she replies, "But Mommy said I will grow tall one day, so I will have to change." She's got me there.

"On that note, I will bid you all farewell." I curtsy this time with Hails joining me.

Merrick needs the last word. "Please give that motherfucker my regards."

"Daddy!" Hails scolds.

I know he's talking about my dad.

I appear unfazed. "Of course, as you wish."

Fallon mouths *I love you*, and I whisper back, "I love you more," before turning on my heel and returning home.

8. Gabriel

Watching my kid smoke a joint from on top of the family mausoleum is something I do frequently in hiding. It's also how I found out my other kid, Mark, was fucking his great-great-grandmother, Darla.

For a dad, catching your kid in such an act is traumatizing. To find him in this position with his great-great-grandmother is alarming and nearly blinding. But as the kids say, love is love and who am I to stand in the way of it?

In fact, he had Darla bent over in that exact spot just earlier this evening. I think Darla suggested that tree on purpose, and Mark, who still only thinks with his dick, agreed. Forever tainting his brother's sacred spot. Siblings will be siblings. It doesn't change even in death.

It's late. Stars twinkle, owls call out to one another, and a murder of crows fly above the newest grave from the other evening.

Earlier today, before Mark banged Darla, Merrick brought his daughter out here to play. She is absolutely precious. I could sit here for hours watching her explore and discover the world for the first time. And today was no different. This afternoon Darla explained the new grave and how her mom will help them transition into the spirit world, and that's how Fallon takes care of Hails; she takes care of the spirits. Her eyes lit up, and chunky cheeks smiled with pride as she declared, "Because my mommy is the best mommy in the world."

Seeing Hails grow up is a gift. Just as I watched my kids after Joanie killed me. Fucking bitch. As I would have rather been by their side while they navigated life. But not everyone gets what they want, unfortunately. But perhaps they do get what they deserve, including her. A good old-fashioned slice and dice. I kicked my heels and shit on her dismembered body parts after they were hidden far, far away. And that fucking bitch Joanie was not coming back in any form with the way they handled her after. And my contribution was simply the cherry on top.

Anyhow, back to watching my boy. Who has turned into a remarkable man and father. Not showing myself after death was a choice to protect my boys from a similar fate, but it seems as if fate was already written for them. Or was my absence the catalyst? Either option is plausible. But to dwell on it doesn't fix it. Trying to make up for it changes nothing. The night with Harper, I had never heard her so honest and blunt, but not in a rude way. It was actually rather cute. And one hundred percent correct. My actions were overbearing, selfish, and self-serving. I wanted to do what I couldn't do for my own kin, and it wasn't right to project that upon her without an invitation. Six simple words: *"I don't need to be saved."* But it's what she meant behind them that has hit me in the most profound way.

Instead of continuing to live, she would rather dance with the unliving? To let her go. To not attempt to do what I wish I could for my children. Shaking my head, I feel sadness and frustration, I've been living in denial and regret, but I will make the most of the circumstances. Scratching my head, I focus on something else she said which penetrated my heart:

predator. Grinning, my teeth prick my bottom lip mischievously, oh, Harper Hayes, that I will gladly be.

I didn't start watching her until she was nearly eighteen. I'm not a groomer and I am not a predator, like she so freely accuses now. The first time I noticed her was when she took refuge in the graveyard's beautiful silence.

Those beautiful slate blue eyes were captivated by their new surroundings. A slight proud smirk adorned her delicate yet confident face, because I know she had to have snuck in. Because Joanie never allowed anyone back here. Harper's long, dark locks swayed as her teeth nibbled on her plump bottom lip. It was at that moment I became captivated. Then several months later, obsessed. The need to always know what she was up to became a compulsion. I would check on her daily. And anytime I saw tears of sadness trickling down her soft cheeks, I wished I had been able to stop them.

When smiles and laughter radiate from her, the entire room lit up and still does. Her quirky personality keeps everything around her interesting. Including her game of chicken with a speeding vehicle.

The girl is beautiful, simply stunning, but it's her personality that holds my attention. Every moment in her presence is a new adventure that I never want to end.

Fuck, I wonder what she's doing right now. And in a blink, I am leaning against the large willow trunk, which is the perfect distance away to give me a full view of her room. Lights are on, curtains open; she never closes until just before her eyes close and her mind drifts into a deep slumber, only to reopen them in the morning after coming back from the magical dreamland she visited that night.

Glancing through the large glass panes with white wooden arches, Harper is lying on her plush area rug. It's one of her favorite spots. Her back arches, she's naked. One hand is squeezing her supple breast as fingers pinch her pert nipple. She's fit, her stomach muscles flex, collarbones catching the light and shadows, as her waist caves in and her chest curves forward. Harper's other arm is reaching forward, between her thighs, and over her bare pussy. I hiss. "Fuck." I reach down my tight jeans, palming my rock-hard cock. Not wanting to be caught with it out, I revert to my teenage years of coming in my pants after a dry hump.

My eyes hood, mesmerized by her beauty. Harper's knees crash together, her movements become more frantic, contorting as her back arches once more. Her mouth opens as her chest moves rapidly. She's coming. And so am I.

Warm cum coats my fingers as her delicious body stills before rising from the comfort of the white shag rug. With red cheeks and disheveled black locks, she inserts three fingers into her mouth, hollowing her cheeks, and sucks her own release off them. This fucking woman is a dream.

With her chest still heaving, I free my hand from my trousers and wipe my mess on the crisp green grass at my feet. Next to the base of the tree, I spot a small pile of pebbles. Which gives me an idea.

Taking a couple between my fingers, I move closer to her window and throw one, then another, startling her. Harper freezes, her fingers still firmly between her pretty pink lips. Eyes widen, immediately sobering her from an orgasmic haze.

Chuckling to myself, proud of my devious behavior, I throw one more and disappear. Giving her a taste of what my predator tendencies could look like.

But also, does no one in this family care about carpal tunnel?

9. Harper

So, I'm a chronic masturbator. Get over it.

But also, what the fuck was that?

I'm not sure if my heart is still racing from coming or from the fear that someone is out there, watching me. Sweat beads on my skin as I sit still on the carpet, in a puddle of my own release, watching myself in the window's reflection. A couple candles flicker, casting shadows along the walls. And completely setting the tone for a *Dateline* episode featuring yours truly.

Fuck, images of previous episodes flash in my vision. I have little time to escape, if any at all. They could be lurking and waiting for my grand escape plan, only to be captured as relief washes over me. Thinking

I am home free, that I have outsmarted the culprit, but really, I am already dead.

I wonder if he will leave me for my friends and family to find, or hide me in the vast foliage surrounding our small town. Everyone will know it was an inside job based on the time of year as the town isn't open yet. The culprit will hide in plain sight, that asshole. As those closest to me mourn, they will cackle.

Oh, shit.

I need to write a will before this all happens. A loud ticking dominates over my rambling thoughts.

Time is ticking.

Crawling on my hands and knees, I scurry to my bedside table and open the drawer as I rummage rapidly through the mess until I find a pen and Post-it note.

Dad,

DO NOT TURN ME INTO MOM. BURY ME. LET ME LIVE A PEACEFUL SECOND LIFE IN ETERNITY!

xx
Harper

Leaving it on the tabletop, visible for Dad to easily find, I reach for the phone next and dial Fallon. It rings four times before she answers. Doesn't she know I am about to die? Where is her sense of urgency?

Frantic, I spit the words out, "I'm coming over!" then hang up.

Yes, on a landline. Google it. I don't have time to explain right now. Things are getting very stressful.

Still on my hands and knees, I poke my head up from next to the bed. My shifty eyes glance around the room, seeing no sign of the person who will end me yet.

Having thrown my clothes in the laundry basket, I maneuver myself to my dresser next. No time for coordination, I grab the first things I see and start wiggling myself into them. With my entire body lying on the floor, my hips shift as my hands pull up a pair of jean shorts at least two sizes too small. Again, no time to care. I get them high enough that they cover my bits, but I'm unable to zip and button them. Next is a white tee with a unicorn on the front. This bastard is also too small. But it covers my tits, so we are good to go.

Though my hair is disheveled, so be it, I jump to my feet and go. The copious amounts of sweat that has accrued on the pads of my feet helps me grip the hardwood floor as I make my way down the dark hallway and very dangerous stairs. Just ask my mother. With both feet, I hop off the bottom step onto the cool tile, and take off toward the front door. Still in the clear.

Turning the doorknob, I yank it back and I am met with nothing. The door doesn't budge, it's locked. No, no, no. The added seconds to unlock it only add additional time for the predator to get me. With shaking hands, I grip the cool brass lock and turn it, but it gets stuck midway. Motherfucker. I put all my weight behind it and finally the click of freedom sounds. Pushing the heavy door open, I could kick my heels if I knew how. My escape to safety is now within reach.

The cool night air is a welcome reprieve for my warm skin. Pumping my arms, my legs move quickly. Tiny pebbles from the long driveway embed themselves in my heels. But none of it matters if the pervert culprit gets me. Yes, I have added pervert to their title, because they clearly were watching me tickle the magical chest.

Our gate is always open and tonight is no different. My chest heaves. I haven't worked out in years, so this is exhausting on my lungs. The annoyance of the tight jean shorts is no more. They have stayed up the entire time, not sabotaging my escape from death. The shirt, properly restricting, but it doesn't matter.

The tall iron gate gets closer and closer. I am almost free. And once it's safe to come back, cleaning out my closet will be at the top of my list of priorities. We can't have this happening again. Oh my Satan, what if I die in this? To be conceded is not in my nature, but this would be a less-than-ideal final look for me. Merrick would have material for centuries.

Rushing through the threshold, I am free. I am safe. Tears of relief follow, knowing this is when the pervert culprit will perhaps get me. An owl hoots. My body jumps followed by a high-pitched scream, and I am off. Rushing across the street, I slip through Fallon's gate, as I usually do, and haul ass up her long driveway. At this point hands are flailing, shoulders jumping, and irrational thoughts stir.

I cross over the donut dick and hear a manic cackle. Merrick Knight.

Glancing up, I find the smug baby daddy leaning over the second-story balcony, grinning from ear to ear. "What the fuck are you wearing?" Asshole.

As a wise woman once said, *middle fingers up, put them sky high*. We've redacted her name, I'm not sure how pleased she'd be being a part of this narrative. But I take her advice and raise them sky high to Merrick as I continue to sprint toward the house.

"Harper. What is going on?" Fallon sees me. She is

already outside, ready to greet me on the large wraparound porch lit by beautiful lanterns.

Waving her off, I plow past her and just before I throw myself through the front door, my feet trip over themselves, catapulting me into the air before quickly and painfully landing on my face. A slow clap commences. No need to look because I already know who it is. I lay in defeat, panting.

"Harper, are you okay?" Fallon asks, concerned. I nod, my face against the ground.

Merrick still claps as he slides in with a follow-up question. "Did you catch your parents banging?"

Nostrils flare. My body tenses in pain. I am never running again.

Peeling myself off their front entrance floor, I ignore him this time. No clever comeback, no smug comment. Instead, I carefully rise to my feet, wipe my knees off, and walk into the library with my head held high. "You have the weirdest friends, my stupid fucking girl." And I can feel his eye roll burning into the back of my head, followed by lips smacking, and I nearly vomit.

Throwing myself onto the plush velvet forest green couch, my body relaxes into a starfish and I have no shame or humility left. Footsteps against the tile become closer and I smile. A brilliant idea crosses my mind. Perhaps it's pure genius or my partial concussion, we will never know, but it will be so much fun.

I'm smiling from ear to ear, eyes open, while my beautiful bestie watches me with worry. Brow furrowed with hands on her hips.

Shrugging my shoulders, like none of this is a big deal, I say, "I heard a noise."

Blinking rapidly at my casual statement, she shakes her head. "Pardon me?"

"It was a loud noise." I bat my lashes at her, pouting my lip and hoping she'll feel sorry for me. Instead, creases form on her forehead.

"I have never seen you run, ever."

She doesn't believe me. "I thought I could be the next episode of *Dateline*."

Merrick interjects. "You are being stranger than usual. It's really fucking annoying."

And he took the vague bait. He hates when people are vague.

"If you must know." I pause to compose myself, then clear my throat before continuing. "I was masturbating, naked on my bedroom floor, as I like to do. Images of your dead father flashing in my mind from the ol' spank bank helped me climax. His long dark locks, rugged but groomed beard against his chiseled jawline. And those hands. It gets me going every time. Then, I heard a noise."

Merrick and his black boot-clad feet jump on top of the coffee table. His finger points directly in my face as he bends at the waist. His eyes are wide, serious and angry. How fun!

"You take that back."

Silence fills the space. Another game of chicken. Who will budge first? Do I tell him how soft his dad's hair is? Or how he likes it pulled? How the feeling of Gabriel's strong hands on my body sends me spinning? My pussy throbs at the thought. I wonder how that man is with his tongue.

Before we get to find out, Fallon bursts out into a fit of laughter. I glance over, alarmed. A wet mark reveals itself on her purple pastel pajama pants. And between giggles, with both hands on her pregnant belly, she wheezes, "I've pissed myself." Then continues on with her hysterical laughter.

Merrick finds none of this amusing, even Fallon's situation, which has my shoulders shaking as I try to hold it in. I love her so much.

"This is out of fucking hand. Both of you have issues. Serious fucking issues."

A tiny gasp follows. "Daddy! No swearing in front of the corpses."

Hails.

"It doesn't count when Daddy is the corpse, baby."

Standing up, adjusting my trendy outfit, I whisper, "Don't worry, your entire bloodline minus the tiny humans, Darla and Mark, repulse me."

Hails yawns, holding her stuffed teddy bear. Walking over to her, I rub her cute bedhead. "Sorry for waking you."

She yawns once more. "It's okay, Harp-Harp."

Looking over my shoulder, Fallon is still giggling at herself, which brings on my own set of giggles. "Thank you and good night." Taking a bow, Hails claps because she is a team player, and I slowly back away and leave, feeling proud of myself and a lot less scared of the pervert culprit who watched me spank my bank.

Dad's car is home by the time I walk back up the drive.

And I am still very terrified. The pervert culprit could still be out here, lurking. Or even inside.

But I must face my fears.

It takes every ounce of power and strength to remove the tee and shorts I wiggled myself into earlier tonight. The candles I had lit have since burned out, drops of wax hardening, and the room is chilled. My chandelier lights the room but even this bright, with nothing to be afraid of in the dark, something feels different.

Tossing my clothes to the corner, because they are definitely seeing the trash can tomorrow, I walk around the quiet space, tapping my finger against my skin. Very peculiar, indeed.

My black velvet curtains are closed shut.

Spinning around, I rush to my nightstand and see my last living will and testament have vanished. Dad wouldn't have found it yet. I catch a glimpse of something on my pillow from my peripheral. Cautiously, I reach for it, gripping the piece of paper between my fingers.

You're so beautiful when you come.
GK x

10. Gabriel

I didn't mean to scare her.

To cause a traumatizing panic was not my intent, yet it still happened. I just needed her to know I was watching and loving every fucking minute of her performance for me. Because in her subconscious, it was.

In leaving the note, I hoped it would ease her near heart attack and partially concussed state. And now, sitting against her plush headboard next to her, I watch while she sleeps. Each breath she takes is a relief. This girl deserves to live a million great lives.

Carefully lifting my hand from my stomach, I slowly reach over, hooking loose pieces of hair and delicately slipping them behind her ear. Eyes flutter under her lids and I wonder what she's dreaming about in that incredible mind.

To reveal myself to her the other night was never my plan. To watch over and protect her was all I had intended to do with my obsession. Or infatuation. But I couldn't let her die. For selfish reasons or not, I always want her here, in this form, not in mine. A ghost. And if to protect meant to reveal, then it had to be done to save this beautiful, complex flower lying next to me.

It was worth it and I would do it a thousand times over.

Looking around her room, a room that I've explored many times, but never from this spot, I note Harper's fireplace is lit, flames flickering to keep my sweet flower warm as she sleeps. White roses and melted candles rest on the mantel. The velvet curtains have stayed closed. She didn't fight it. But I hate that one of her favorite places is now ruined, all because I needed to toy with my sweet flower.

More melted candles line the floor and decorate her dresser. Vases of black calla lilies sit on the bedside tables next to me and her. Her room is minimal yet elegant. The beautiful chandelier hanging in the center is the perfect finishing touch. A hint of black to draw the eye, to create further contrast. This is her retreat.

Her safe space. Where Harper can be herself. Pour her soul out into the journal hiding beneath her bed or having a finger bang. The real Harper Hayes lives in this room. Where she keeps her secrets safe and vulnerability hidden. What others see is a masked version of herself.

And I promise to love all thirty-seven versions of her.

I know. The L-word already? But don't forget, I have known her for years. She has kept me captivated since the very first moment and will until our very last. I won't say it to her, not yet. She needs time to catch up, and I will give her that time and all the time she needs if it means she picks me too.

I cherish and worship her. I am loyal and possessive of her. "I will give you a life worth living if you let me," I whisper out loud, finishing my thoughts.

Joanie destroyed me. Killed me. And Harper has brought me back to life.

Glancing over at my Sleeping Beauty with her raven hair cascading over bare shoulders, urges take over and I am now floating above her. Goosebumps slowly rise from my nearness of her. I am only inches away and her lips part. Perhaps subconsciously she senses me. Leaning my face forward, I tickle her face with my beard, lightly brushing it over her skin.

Harper shivers. My dick hardens at her reaction, and sadly, he is a captive in my tight jeans, fighting his restrictions.

Like father like son, if you know what I mean. And yes, you felt that cheeky wink because I definitely did it when I said that.

Then, an idea occurs. Smirking, I give in to the temptation of it. "Come out and play with me, Harper Hayes."

Her body shifts under her blankets, but her eyes do not awaken.

"Sleeping Beauty. It's time to play," I whisper softly against her cheek, yet she still doesn't stir.

Lowering myself to stand next to her on the side of the bed, I slide my arms underneath her and the blankets, and lift her bridal style against my chest. More shivers follow as her body tucks into mine. Carefully, we leave her room. I peer out into the hall. The house is dark. Not a creature is stirring, not even her dad's dick inside of her dead mother.

Too much? It's not like it isn't true.

Being a ghost has its perks. I don't need to worry about creaks in the floor or bumping into walls. Well, that last bit depends on if you have a person in your arms, like I do now. But typically, I can float on through.

Bringing us downstairs, I take us through her grand kitchen. It's beautiful. I loved cooking when I was alive. She has a gas stove, it's black with copper fixtures. The overhead fan is a matching copper and it is the showstopper of the space. If Harper would like it, I would happily cook for her here. Make her some of her favorite meals, and ones that were once mine. I can picture her, all adorable, sitting on the counter, swinging her sneaker-clad feet, while I feed her samples of my latest creation. This girl could destroy me. But I hope she doesn't.

A large window sits above the black farmhouse kitchen sink, overseeing the most impressive garden. Large trees decorate the entire property, wildflowers, and creeks. It's peaceful. I have always found it most curious about why she would choose the cemetery to escape in.

Her family's home is grand, but eclectic in terms of decor. Each room uniquely themselves, their own personality. From outside, this white Victorian home seems like it should be gothic and cryptic. Considering the morgue in the basement and death surrounding it. But it is uniquely perfect. And how it should be.

Another large fireplace is against the far wall in the kitchen, a large mantel on top and filigree engraved into the wood decorating the sides. Two cream chairs and a small table around it. A perfect spot for a peaceful nightcap.

I would like to share this home with her. Make it ours. To sit with her in those chairs after a long day. Or to have her resting in my lap and against my chest as I massage the stress out of her neck. It's where she hides it.

Opening the back door and stepping outside, the comfort of fresh air greets us. Harper, in only a pair of thin panties, shivers once more. I am tempted to hold her closer, but it would only make it worse.

Acres of green space offers itself as the backdrop to the game we are going to play. Walking on the dark stone path, we pass her treasured flower garden. Since her mom's unexpected passing, Harper has kept the flowers flourishing. It keeps her connected to her mother. She spends hours ensuring everything is perfect and all her babies remain healthy. Those on death's door, she clips and brings inside to her room, surrounding herself in them during their final days. Harper is always respectful, even when it comes to nature.

You know the old saying, you can take the girl out of the morgue but you can't take the mortician out of the girl.

The winding path leads us farther past the garden

and lush trees arch overhead. A hidden gazebo reveals itself. They have a few within the property. Green vines wrap around each dark wooden pillar and meet on the domed roof. A large weeping willow gives us a beautiful backdrop as I place Harper gingerly down on the long wooden bench. Her arms drape over either side and her mind is still at rest.

Leaning over her, I whisper once more, "Come play with me, Harper Hayes." And this time she hears me. Her eyes move more frantically under her lids as her beautifully exposed body stirs.

And I vanish, though I still keep watch over her.

HARPER

Chills tickle me. Why am I so cold?

My eyes flutter open as my head rolls against something hard.

I don't understand. Attempting to roll over, I am met with no resistance and fall hard onto the ground. "Shit. Why am I outside?" My voice is groggy from being rudely awoken from a fabulous sleep. It exhausted me, from masturbating to the panic and running then falling. After getting home, I immediately crashed the second my head hit the soft pillow. But a bed and pillow are no longer where I lay.

Pushing my body up, I rise to my feet and look around. It's still night, tiny insects sing and owls hoot. Relief washes over me. At least I am home. Then I wonder, did I sleepwalk out here? Was I that relaxed? This is so bizarre.

Stepping down to the stone path, it's freezing against my feet. Nights are always cold in Port Canyon, and this night is no different.

"If I catch you, I keep you," is whispered into my ear. My heart drops into my stomach. I spin rapidly on my heel, terrified. But the space is empty. This makes little sense. Swallowing, my mouth is dry as my breathing becomes heavy. I scan the gazebo once more before turning back around. Taking two more steps, I am stopped as the voice returns with the same words. "If I catch you, I keep you."

My lips tremble, fingers shake. And my *Dateline* episode is now reaching its peak. The mind is no longer in control, my body's instincts is to take over and my legs move of their own accord, making me run yet again. This is so fucking rude. Thankfully, genetics didn't bless me with larger bosoms, these ones are manageable for running topless.

Taking off, I plow down the path, weaving around the curves, and tempted to dart through the shrubs, but resist. Just as my garden comes into view, I smile. Home free, baby. But boy am I wrong.

Something cold wraps itself around my bare stomach, stopping me from my frenzied escape. I'm stuck. Unable to move. My back is against something hard as another cold feeling wraps itself around my throat. A heart that was once in the pit of my stomach now beats swiftly in my ears. Tears prick my eyes from the adrenaline crash.

I attempt to jolt forward, but the hold on me tightens. Breathing is more restricted as I gasp for air. A whisper follows, tickling my ear. "That was a beautiful show you put on for me earlier."

Gabriel.

I'm safe. But curious. I don't fight anymore. Relaxing into his tight embrace, waiting for what's coming next. I should actually kick him in the dick and balls for what he did earlier, but I'm not entirely sure ghosts feel the same impact as humans do with that move. Don't worry, I will get my revenge once I sort all the logistics out. But right now, I am genuinely intrigued to see where this is going to stop it.

"One day, I will chase you through these woods. You will try to hide, but I will always find you." Chills run down my spine. But I don't speak. "Are you scared?" he questions. I shake my head no. And he is quick to respond. "You should be."

Squeezing my neck tighter, his other hand moves and his fingers find the top of my panties. Gabriel's fingers tease me. "Let me see you." I want to watch, but can't while he is still in his hidden form.

"I like you bossy," is all he says before spinning me around and throwing me over his shoulder. And he is no longer hidden. I have the best view. Gabriel's fit ass in these tight jeans. Come to Mommy. It's perfection. Just as I drool shamelessly, a sharp sting from a slap on my ass brings me back to the present. We are off the fucking ground. Where are we going?

Swinging my arms over, I hold on to his ass for dear life. This fucker better not drop me. My living will and testament is no longer in plain view for my father to find. Instead, it's tucked between pages of my journal.

I feel his body chuckling against mine. Doesn't he know it's rude to laugh at a scared, naked person? My eyes roll. And somehow, he knows. Gabriel slaps my ass once more and this time my pussy tingles, too. Well played, good sir, well fucking played.

Landing back on the ground, he throws me onto the bed of grass. His body hovers over mine and I am so fucking horny.

This man does things to me I have never experienced before. Twice in one night causing me such panic, but then being turned on... by said panic. Reaching up, I grab his face between my hands, and he doesn't resist, allowing me to pull him closer. Our faces meet, millimeters apart. My lips close the space, meeting his. As they connect, all oxygen leaves my lungs as the universe sucks it from me. The tips of my fingers tingle with excitement and my toes curl. Gabriel's tongue slips past my lips and mine meets his. A sexy game of tonsil hockey is now in session. I can feel my panties becoming more moist and I wish his fingers would slip underneath to play with me more, but they don't. Instead, they circle over the top. A moan escapes him as he feels how wet I am, causing me to melt further. I could eat his moans and groans all day if he let me.

Moving his hand, he replaces it with his hard dick, which is pressing against his jeans. I want more, so much fucking more. But I decide to take it slow. Wrapping my legs around his fit waist, I grind my pelvis against his, giving him my moans and desire. Because, ladies, we can't give it all away, not before a first date, at least.

Before we get too carried away, I pull back. Opening my eyes, they meet his. This man is so beautiful, I could stay like this forever. But before my body betrays me any further, I need to change the subject. Keeping our deep eye contact with one another, my sexy predator, who is rocking a pussy-wetting man bun, tickles his nose against mine. Damn him, I will not give in yet. Silence surrounds us, with the exception of my beating heart. So, I break it. This question has been on my mind since the moment he mentioned his death. From knowing Joanie over the years, before she died, I've been assuming. And I need to know.

"How did she murder you?"

11. Gabriel

Since the moment the words left her lips, I was stunned.

Admiring her nearly naked form, I am captivated by her beauty, as if it were the first time all over again. And it's at this moment I decide I never want to keep anything from her. If she wants the truth, the answers, she will get them.

"You're cold. Let me take you inside."

Harper shakes her head. "Tell me. I want to know. Please." Her blue-slate eyes are filled with battling emotions.

I brush the hair off her face and reassure her, "I promise I will. But first we need to get you inside where it's warm. Please," using the same trick back on her. While brushing my lips down her jaw and onto her neck. Her legs squeeze tighter around me as her head nods against my face, accepting the compromise like the good fucking girl she is.

Scooping her into my arms, I squeeze her tight in return. The smell of sweet florals and marshmallows tickles my senses. She is my home.

Harper's arms wrap around my neck, and her thumbs mindlessly toy with the lose hair which has strayed from my bun. Moving us quickly through the yard and back through the house, it's still quiet. The dancing flames of the fireplace greet us, returning to her room. Gingerly, placing her back into her bed, Harper's lips move seductively against the stubble along my neck. Her teeth nip at me while her pelvis begins to grind. My cock reacts, knowing she owns him.

Gentle hands wrap around her head as I pull back slowly. I don't want her to feel rejected. Soft eyes greet her, full of lust and shining brightly. "First, it's time for your bedtime story, my beautiful girl." For all the years I have been admiring her from afar, I have never seen Harper with another man intimately. When, not if, when this happens, I want her to be sure because once she has me, I am never leaving.

Blowing out a sigh of slight annoyance, she rolls

her eyes and playfully pushes my chest. "Fine. But only because this is a bedtime story I need to hear."

Unwrapping myself from around her, she also lets me free, begrudgingly. Pulling her comforter up, I tuck it under her chin and kiss her forehead lightly before lying next to her.

The dancing flames draw me in as my mind contemplates where to start.

"The beginning." Turning to look at Harper and her cute little smile, she continues. "The key to a great story is starting it at the beginning, so we understand how we got the here, to the now, and in this moment."

Brilliant and beautiful. I am done for with this one. But I already knew that and I didn't run. And I still won't now. "You're right." Tilting my head against the headboard, I blow out a loud sigh while shaking my head slightly. I haven't relived many of these memories since my first years of death. I was angry. So fucking angry for a very long time. Followed by deep hurt and selfishness, self-pity, shame, and loathing. Then I saw her and nothing else mattered.

"When the town opened all those years ago, some friends from college and I decided to see what all the hype was about. Port Canyon, the spooky town, closed off to the world with ghosts and curses. It screamed fun to the underdeveloped male teenage brain. If you were to ask Fallon, she could attest to this. Port Canyon captivates you the moment you enter. Time froze all those years ago when the founding families, such as yours and Joanie's, first developed it. The old clock tower to the cobblestones and candle-lit streetlights. Narrow roads and cozy shops with the bell that rings when the door opens. Time has changed nothing except for the copious amounts of weed that kid grows in his yard for my son. That wasn't there before, or if it was, not in such a quantity." I chuckle, smiling at the memory.

"That night is the night that changed it all for me. She was standing with some friends at the end of the driveway of the Knight compound. The gate was open, and they were all laughing at something funny. Her long brown hair was pin-straight, draped over her shoulders. She was wearing a sky-blue jumpsuit, the neckline cut down the center to just above the belly button, exposing a peek of her chest. Sitting in the back seat, I slammed my hand against my friend's seat and demanded he stop. I had to meet that girl. And he did. I walked up, cocky, with my long hair flowing freely, and interpreted the girl talk to introduce myself. The girl of my dreams, who stole my heart with one look, rejected me, shrugging me off, and wanting nothing to do with me. Squealing tires pulled my attention back to my friends. Burnt rubber smelt horribly against the stone as they sped away, leaving me."

Harper yawns, loudly, and I'm nearly positive it was on purpose. Is my beautiful girl jealous?

Sarcastically, I retort, "You said every good story starts at the beginning," smirking over at her.

Harper bats her lashes at me. "I lied. Now please, get to the good part."

I choke on her words. "My death?"

Realization follows. Regret washes over her face as she becomes tongue-tied for words. "I didn't mean that. I just. Fuck, I'm so sorry, Gabriel. Your death was and is tragic."

Perhaps I should make her sweat just a little. Tapping my finger against my chin, I question playfully. "Are you jealous?"

All blood rushes out of her face, lips move, but no words come out. And maybe I did catch my little minx in a fit of jealousy, after all.

A fake laugh follows, and her eyes look anywhere but in my direction. Glistening, shit, I've embarrassed her. *Shit*, again.

Reaching my hand over, my body shifts to its side, facing her as my thumb rubs her cheek. "It's okay, Harper. I'm sorry. I know you didn't mean any harm."

I need to remember my playful flirting is all so new to her. She is only used to sarcastic wit only being thrown her way from my son or a surface-level love from her father.

"Okay, let's skip to the good part. Even though it was love at first sight, it didn't stay that way. I stayed after that night. Changed my entire life to be with Joanie. It was magical at first, everything was so new, including learning about the town's history, legends, and the family legacy. I fucking loved being a part of it." Pausing, I gather my thoughts, because as hard as it is for her to listen, it's even harder to tell my story. All jokes aside, because those just mask the hurt.

"I ignored all the warning signs. I poured all my energy into the boys. I was so excited to start our family and she hated them. She hated us. At first, I thought it was post-partum depression, so I begged for her to see someone about it, to talk to a doctor. Anything she needed, I would have done or supported her. Joanie became the priority. But it didn't matter. For months, nothing changed and her resentment grew, not just toward the boys, as it really peaked after Merrick, but toward me. But as time went on, it became clear that she was just a fucking bitch."

Harper breaks into a fit of laughter, not expecting that diagnosis. But it's true. I read books, did research, talked to the doctor and other moms. This was not post-partum. This was resting bitch, without the resting.

"All her time spent was in the graveyard, from sunrise to sunset. I would try to bring the boys out, meet her for a picnic lunch, and she would only yell at us for disturbing her day and the process in the cemetery. She was meticulous. And at first, I admired her dedication to nurturing the spirits and wanting to help and protect them. But as time went on it took precedence over family. From dusk until dawn she stayed out back, even the afterlife was beginning to lose their patience with Joanie. It was around then her controlling nature started to shine through. Her obsession to being worshipped by them stunk, only pushing the ghosts away. Our boys used to cry endlessly for their mom until they didn't. And it annoyed her less that way. As time went on, we all lived a separate life to Joanie. We just existed under the same roof but experienced two very different realities."

Moving closer to Harper, I take my hand off her cheek and rest my head on her covered chest. Tiny fingers pull out my hair tie, before they begin to rake through my hair, scratching my scalp in comfort.

"I never understood why. She hated her family. But to be left with two boys, it made little sense to me.

Joanie didn't want to give up her birthright to the family she created when the time came. She got selfish, greedy, and controlling. The spirits, as you know, picked up on that and became resentful. Rightfully. As miserable as she was with us, she was twice as bad with them because she was required to actually speak to them, especially the new ones who she was required to help transition over." Tapping my fingers against Harper's blanket like a drumroll, I tee up the good part.

"In killing me. She knew it would kill her kids. Leaving her as the sole heir. Never losing her status or responsibilities. She saw the three of us as her biggest threat. I even changed my last name for her, happily. I loved my family."

We lay in silence for a moment, allowing me to gather my thoughts. "Joanie and your father were friends. She used him to gain access to your basement. Harper, you have to know your dad is innocent in all this. Dougie boy has been naughty, but not when it comes to me." I am yanked back. Harper's fingers tightly grip my hair and pull it, hard. I yelp, submitting to my queen. "I deserved that. But, please, I need my hair," I joke.

"Joanie stole an entire bottle of embalming fluid. And later that same night loaded a syringe with one hundred units ready to inject into my veins. We didn't sleep in the same room; I stayed in the boys' wing. There was never a reason to lock the door. She hated us, but wasn't homicidal. Until she was."

I feel Harper freeze under me. Giving her a moment, I allow her to process everything, until she surprises me by saying, "This is your *Dateline* episode."

Audibly, I chuckle, my chest rumbling. "Yes, I suppose it is." This fucking girl. I love her more and more with each day. But I have no clue what a Dateline is.

"Joanie ended up sneaking into my room that night with two loaded syringes. One for my heart, the other for my neck. I was dead within minutes. It was a silent death. I kept my eyes closed. I refused to let her be the last thing I saw. The last real image embedded into my memory would be my boys. My boys who I watched each night, sleeping in their beds. I checked in on them every night, regardless of their age. It was so cold as the fluid spread. Then, I was gone. As time went on, Mark found love and left the town. Curse be damned, it was his first excuse to leave, and he took it, but the town and Joanie indirectly got him. And you know Merrick's story. He could never mask his pain until after death. Now he uses his wit. But she got hers.

I only wish her pain lasted longer, but it doesn't matter. She's gone..."

Before I can finish, Harper interjects. "And now you can be a family reunited."

I blame myself. I should have removed the boys from that place long ago. Protected them and myself better. They both died because of me. I am a coward. If they hate me when I face them, it would kill me ten times over. So, I change the subject.

"Harper. I am unliving proof that your mom could still come back from this. If we let Fallon help her. Darla would need to guide her, because that's how she helped me. It was harder to enter my spirit, ghost form, but it's possible. Darla could show her."

She swallows, her words quiet. "Yeah. Maybe."

As long as her father keeps her mom here, it won't happen. To get her hopes up, just to be destroyed? I get it.

Changing the subject back, I continue. "So that is the exciting story of my grand finale." Warm lips kiss the top of my head, and my soul, or what I have left of it, melts deeper. To comfort me? It's been decades since I have felt compassion like that, and damn have I missed it.

Harper's body shifts, getting comfortable beneath

me, before heavy breathing follows. She's out, my notoriously heavy sleeper.

I just bared it all to her. And she didn't run. I exposed a secret or two and she just listened. With no judgement.

It has lifted a massive weight off my shoulders, but I hope it has not burdened hers in silence.

12. Harper

Strolling through the peaceful cemetery, the sun is setting, and the sky is filled with beautiful hues of oranges and red. Soon the mountainscape will hide these radiant colors and give us the darkness our town thrives on. I love my home.

It's been a couple of days since Gabriel told me about his death. I was shocked, comforted, and equally vulnerable hearing his story as he was telling it. The topic of my mother is one I actively avoid with others, but I didn't coward away. Gabriel told me he *knows* what Dad does with Mom, without saying it. And instead of judging, to my face, he tried to help with his own story. A story he didn't need to tell me, but did. The entire evening held a deeper meaning, which I am still processing and trying to understand. And the biggest question of them all is: why me?

Why has he now decided to show himself after decades of seclusion? This isn't like Merrick and Fallon. It's the polar opposite: no taunting, no sleep tongue fucking, or mixed signals because he's a giant child. But like Merrick, Joanie is at the center of why we are all in this impasse. She killed her boys, directly or indirect. She chose the fate of Fallon and me before we even realized it.

One decision changed the entire course of history. And did my dad know the bottle was missing? How could he not? It's rarely used, so did he condone it? I want to be so mad at him. But then I wouldn't have my best friend or her babies. Darla wouldn't have found Mark, the graveyard wouldn't be thriving, and I wouldn't have met Gabriel. Don't get my running thoughts twisted, I am certainly not putting Joanie on a pedestal for her actions, screw that shrew. Is this what they mean by the butterfly effect?

Fuck. This is getting really deep, but graveyard strolls let me untangle my mind and attempt to comprehend the many layers of my life. Don't feel bad for me. We all have our shit. This is just how I decompress from mine. Besides playing chicken with a car. One time. Let's not keep bringing that up. I am a newfound thrill seeker, remember? If I keep saying it out loud it helps, okay? And it was a problem solved until Gabriel Knight dropped this major truth bomb on me.

Speaking of our main man. Gabriel, the one with the sexy long, soft hair and rugged features. The sound of his voice makes my panties moist, and never mind those strong hands decorated with gold jewelry and protruding veins when he grips me tightly. That magnificent specimen has been missing for days. Because he is nothing less than a predatorial gentleman. We cannot forget, Gabriel still toyed with me outside before telling his story. Leaving me nearly naked on a bench before seductively awakening me, he chased me down the stone path, leaving me fearful and slightly aroused. Okay, very aroused. My pussy ached for him to toy with me further before revealing himself. But alas, he is playing the pussy card tease well.

Anyhow, it would appear that he has given me the space and time to absorb everything, not rushing my processing process of it all. The bombs dropped were rather significant after all.

Kicking my feet through the long grass off the well-worn paths of the cemetery, I have been mindlessly wandering for ages. Attempting to gather my thoughts and feelings, instead of allowing them to haunt and taunt me as my eyes close for the night. Taking in my surroundings, I notice I am in a part of the cemetery rarely frequented. This is where spirits go to hide when they wish to be left alone. Where Gabriel hid from us and his family. A wave of sorrow washes over me. To be alone, isolated, by choice, thinking you are protecting your kin to find out it was all for nothing. It's a sad existence to have. Then realization floods over me. It's wildly similar to the life I have been living. I've only gained Fallon as a friend in the past few years. Before that, I led a secluded life, getting lost in the morgue or here. Avoiding everything.

Scratching my head, I smirk, proud of myself and us. That's another few hundred saved. Thank you, team. You're really coming in clutch. I should have acknowledged your lurking years ago. This would have solved a lot of my fucking issues, it seems.

Taking a deep breath of the clean mountain air into my lungs, my ribs expand and as I exhale, my mind feels so alive. It's decided I am going to take life by the balls, squeeze them, and make it my bitch.

"Are you here?" I shout into the now looming night's sky. The gorgeous colors are fading away, which is ironic, because a bright light has ignited in me.

Glancing from left to right, there's no sign of my Gabriel.

Oh fuck.

He isn't mine. I am not a predator. I do not own him. He is free to come and go as he pleases. But I do wonder if he is lurking about like you lot have been. Just in case, I project my internal thoughts into the universe, hoping he can't resist. "You're doing something to me. And I don't know if I like it or not. You are making me evaluate my life and things I had suppressed many full moons ago."

Still nothing, rude. Come on, Gabriel, take the bait.

I continue. "Your story made me realize how short life really is. How it can be taken from you without a second thought. When Mom died, I was a teen and grief overpowered my logic. The bridge helped me find answers. It did things to me, but at what it could have cost me, it was stupid. Or was it? Because it led me to you?" Blowing out a sigh, I shake my head as shivers tickle down my spine. "I crave the thrill. And now that thrill is you. Not knowing if you're here or not, or what you will do next? That's what gives me excitement. That's what makes my heart beat out of my chest. Last night is what I crave more of. That is my thrill. You. My personal sexy predator."

The truth and vulnerability bomb has now been dropped and Gabriel is nowhere to be seen. And because of that my mind will race tonight, replaying the perceived rejection on repeat until my eyes finally give in to the sparkling sleep dust.

"Ah, so he told you?" Darla pops up, smiling with a twinkle in her eye, which startles me. My body jumps and my feet trip over themselves, causing me to fall backward, landing on the hard cold ground. Fingers grip the crisp grass as I stare up at her, shocked.

Concerned, I question, "How much have you heard?"

She chuckles, all cutesy, before revealing the dreaded answer. "Everything." This is exactly like falling on ice, then looking around hoping no one else witnessed such an embarrassment. And in this case, someone has and I am mortified.

My face winces. "Why?"

Her head shakes. "I bet the entire graveyard heard you, dear. You were yelling rather loudly."

"How long have you known? You said 'so he told you.'"

Darla's finger shakes at me. "It doesn't matter. But it's been some time."

Because we are both telling the truth, this just spits out from between my lips. My mind no longer controls me. "I know about you and Mark." As soon as I say it, my hands cover my mouth.

"There was no way Fallon would not tell you, dear. Of course you know. But you know who doesn't? Merrick. And I would like to keep that boy clueless a bit longer. It makes for better sex, knowing at any moment he could pop up at his tree for a smoke and Mark has me bent over, fucking me into oblivion."

Moving my hands from my mouth to my ears, I don't want to hear it. She's a grandmother figure to me. And nobody needs to picture their grandmother fucking, or getting fucked. Nope, this is just another potential therapy bill.

"And now you can experience the same thrill," she adds.

Holding one hand out at her to stop, I say, "Darla. I'm going to vomit if you continue down this tunnel."

Waving me off, she doesn't care. "Dear, if you think the chase is exciting, wait until he finally claims you."

"Why do you know all of this?" I am simply mortified.

Winking, she grins. "I enjoy watching."

Glazing over her last comment, I ask, "What about my dad?"

And she doesn't mince her words. "You need to talk to him. Tell him how you feel and how his actions impact you. He has been greedy long enough. It's time he considers you and your feelings now, dear. Has he even talked to you about the ceremony? Passing the mortician responsibilities fully onto you at the next full moon?"

I don't respond.

"So, let's add neglectful under greedy. And before you ask, yes, I believe he knew exactly what happened to the embalming fluid and that he was too much of a coward to stop it. Just like he is cowering now, inside of your mother's cold pussy." Darla pauses, meanwhile I wince at the visual her words have given, yet she continues, allowing the words to sink in further. "And lastly, don't fight it, dear. Gabriel."

"I don't want to be his redemption project either. He told me so much, it made me wonder..." My mind drifts off into a thousand different directions and theories.

"You aren't. You are his one chance of real happiness. And look how far you have come since he's entered your life." Her words hit. And my body falls backward onto the ground. Looking up at the night sky, stars twinkle at me brightly and my eyes water.

All right, family, do you have time for another session, because my mind is completely jumbled now.

13. Gabriel

I heard it all.

Even Darla's bit about watching and being bent over by my kid. I accidentally saw them once or twice. They are exhibitionists with no boundaries. More power to them, but there are things in my life I was never meant to see, and my kid's dick impaling her old lady vagina would be on that list. And perhaps we should add voyeurism to their repertoire. Whatever works for them, I suppose.

But the reason I didn't show myself to Harper was because she needed to sort through everything I left her with herself. I didn't want to influence or hinder her processing. Darla jumping in when she did was the much-needed nudge Harper needed. I just hope this didn't push her too far away.

Standing over her, I watch as her chest rises slowly. Lips are parted, breathing is shallow, her long dark hair is fanned out on her silk pillow. Absolutely stunning. My cock hardens against my pants. Reaching down, instead of adjusting him, I unzip myself, pulling him out. Father like son, we love playing when they are asleep.

Gripping my cock, my thumb teases the tip as precum leaks out. Harper's angelic state gets me so horny. She is a goddamn saint. Porcelain skin, with dark hair surrounding her. The most perfect set of tits I've ever seen. Barely a handful each, beautifully on display, just for me. A fire cracks as wood turns to ash, the smell of fresh florals surrounding us. And I truly believe they made this one for me. Joanie gave me my boys, but Harper has given me love.

Reaching my free hand out, I grip her hard nipple, causing my Sleeping Beauty to stir but not waken. Goosebumps rise and my cock twitches at her reaction to me. I need to mold her pussy. My hand can work wonders, but my cock would much prefer being inside her. And when unable, a pocket pussy made of the shape of her.

Fisting my cock harder, I pump myself leisurely at first. The slow build is half the fun. The anticipation excites me. What I would do to tickle her neck with my lips right now. To wrap my tongue around her nipples, teasing the most sensitive spot until she can't take it. Until she gives in to her darkest desires with me. For her to wrap her legs around my neck as I kiss her swollen, needy lips. As she aches for a release only I can give her. Because my needy girl is a chronic masturbator, but it's not the same. A moment of pleasure versus hours of what I can give her.

I need to feel my tip pounding into her cervix. Her walls clench around me as I move slowly inside of her, rubbing against her sensitive spots. Exploring what she desires and craves, then giving in to it. Letting her feel euphoria. Harper deserves to be spoiled. To sit on my face until I see the holy light once more.

My eyes close, daydreaming of all the possibilities we will have together. Pumping faster, I cannot contain myself much longer. Tightness tingles in my balls. My hips move faster as my head falls back. Glancing down, I position my cock over her captivating body as my release decorates her chest. Ropes of cum shoot out as my stomach clenches. Unable to hold back, I move to her lips. I need to see my cum dripping off her sexy, pouty, pink lips.

Tremors tremble throughout my body. As the last bit of cum releases, I squeeze my girth and shake what's dripping off my tip onto my beauty, who is decorated so fucking perfectly for me.

Releasing Harper's nipple, I take a step back. My body freezes, dick in hand, as I am continuously captivated by this creature before me. And before I can tuck myself back into my trousers, she stirs.

"I knew you were here the entire time." Her admission shocks me. She didn't awaken to my touch once.

"Then why didn't you stop me? Or say something?" I question.

Harper's eyes flutter open, my cum glistening beautifully on her lips. She licks it, keeping her eyes on me the entire time, only leaving some to continue dripping down her face and onto her pillow. Moans follow as she savors my release before going on. "Because I liked it."

Her words cause my cock to twitch in my hand. But before we can get too carried away, I need to ease her mind. She struggled to fall into her deep slumber and that killed me. Knowing I was part of the cause of her discomfort. So, I clear my throat, adverting my eyes, because I am a male who is still getting accustomed to exploring and divulging such truths and honesty in person, rather than in my head.

"At first, you were my redemption story. My chance to get it right one more fucking time. But you are so much more than that to me. Since the day I started watching you, I knew you were more. But my need to save and protect you was because I couldn't do the same for Mark and Merrick. You have always gotten me hard, made my heart beat when I thought it was void, and caused butterflies to flutter in my stomach anytime I saw you. The thought of losing you killed me. So, I had to save you. Protect and keep you safe. Always."

Fear of rejection immediately follows. This could go either way, and I am terrified. I haven't felt this way since, well, ever. I never thought Joanie would reject me that night all those years ago. It was easy. And reflecting back, there was a reason for that, we were never meant to be. But Harper, she holds the cards. She is my forever.

Her lips crash against mine. Passion ignites and devotion takes over. I will forever be devoted to this beautiful creature. Relief washes over me and my shoulders relax, arms wrap around her, as her tiny fingers unbutton my trousers.

"Never stop chasing me. Protecting and seeking me. I like when we play that game. But I will mess you up if you do me dirty, Gabriel Knight. Do not test me. I can be mean." I want to laugh and call her out for being so fucking adorable, but I resist this time.

Because I love when she gets all firm and assertive, and I hope to see more of it.

HARPER

Unfastening his tight jeans, my fingers grip the waistband and I yank them down his strong thighs. His cock springs free once more, and Gabriel doesn't wear underwear. My insides melt further into oblivion for this man. His muscles flex as I jump off the bed next to him. He turns to face me as I drop to my knees, without a second thought, because I need him in my mouth. The taste of cum on my lips was just an appetizer. I need it all.

Softly, his fingers tickle under my chin, and tilting my head up, I meet his bright beautiful eyes. "Are you sure?" I understand the question is larger than just three words. Once this happens, we cannot go back from it. We are all in. Consequences be damned. I nod, absolutely sure. Gabriel smirks, his cheekbones rising and showing off more of his sexy attributes.

Excitement floods my stomach as tiny wings tickle around.

Truth be told, I know this will come to a shock too many of you, but I have never sucked a dick before.

Yes, I know. Pick those jaws off the ground because your girl hasn't a fucking clue what to do next.

Gabriel grabs ahold of his giant cock, which is huge, like massive. Lots of girth. How is this going to fit? My breath hitches, eyes widen. What have I gotten myself into?

"That's it, my beauty. Open those sexy lips for me," he encourages. My teeth bite the inside of my cheek, and he paints my pout with precum, causing me to melt further into his spell, happily.

Mustering up my courage once more, I open my mouth. Relaxing my jaw, he steadily works himself inside of my mouth. I gag instantly. I'm embarrassed. And he notices. Gabriel's soft hand gingerly cups my cheek. "It's okay. I love hearing all your sounds." His reassurance gives me the confidence to continue.

"Tap my thigh if it gets to be too much. I'll stop, I swear it." My hands grip his legs and I nod yes, one time, in acknowledgment.

"That's my good girl. Do you know how fucking sexy you look right now? With my cock in your mouth, lashes brushing against your soft cheeks, worshiping me." I get shy, wanting to hide. No one has ever called me sexy before.

"I can't wait to worship you in return, beauty."

My thumb draws circles on his exposed skin. He's

cool to the touch, it's refreshing. Gabriel hisses and pride washes over me. I like that I have the ability to make him react like that. "You hold all the power." His words echo in my head, as if he were just in my mind.

Relaxing my throat, I gag once more, eyes watering as I let him in farther. Gabriel's hand moves from my face to my hair, gripping it at the base of my skull. He doesn't hold back. Once in far enough, his pelvis moves and as my eyes drift up, I find his hooded, lust-filled, and captivated by the sight before him.

Gabriel wastes no time fucking my face into oblivion, and I love it. His words are rough as he repeats, "Mine." It makes my pussy throb. He owns me.

As I attempt to breathe, my lungs contract. I am unable to get any oxygen to them. More gagging ensues as tears stream down my cheeks. Stars begin to flash with each blink of my eyes. Gabriel is choking me with his cock, and I love it. I could black out at any given moment and the realization causes my heart to start beating faster inside my ears. What a rush.

Just before my body falls limp, Gabriel pulls out. My lungs gasp for air and life is renewed. I leave my tongue out, resting over my bottom lip, waiting for his release to coat me, but it doesn't follow. Instead, his panty-soaking man hands grip around my waist as he hoists me up, before tossing me playfully onto the bed.

It's all so effortless with him. I bounce twice before relaxing into the soft sheets and mattress, giggling in a horny daze.

Gabriel reaches up, pulling his thick mane out of his man bun. It cascades down in beautiful waves. Wasting no time, his pants follow as he kicks them off. His shirt is next. He pulls it off over his head, exposing his 'they should be illegal' pectorals. Dark hair decorates his chest and abdomen, with a thin trail leading my gaze back to his hard cock, which is freely bobbing around.

"Are you sure?" he asks the same question once more.

And without hesitation I answer, "Yes."

Another fun fact, which we briefly touched on earlier: I haven't had dick in many full moons. I am basically a born-again virgin, so this should be fun.

Steadying himself on the bed, his cool fingers hook the hem of my panties and slowly pull them down my exposed legs. I watch as he bites his lip once my pussy becomes exposed. And at the same time I wonder what his flavor saver would look like coated in my release.

Before I am able to further fantasize, he tosses my panties over his shoulder and bends down, crashing his lips into mine. Gabriel's strong arms are braced on either side of me while his cock teases me. He is grinding his hips against mine. Instinct takes over as my legs wrap around his waist, and my heels dig into his tight ass as I rock against him in return.

His cock lines up with my entrance, his ass flexes under my feet, and, with one movement, he invades. My back arches off the bed. The intrusion is painful. My face winces, but I try my best to not make it noticeable. But it doesn't work. Gabriel's lips break away from mine. His voice is husky, seductive, and deep when he asks, "Are you…"

But before he can finish that thought, I interrupt frantically. "No. It's just been a while."

He grins, confessing something in return. "Me too." And I immediately melt further into him.

Gabriel's head falls onto my chest. His lips pepper kisses along my collarbone, followed by his tongue sneaking out, licking the dried cum he had left on me only moments prior. And I ask, "Is it good, baby?"

He chuckles, breaking away from my skin for only a second to respond. "Yours would taste better." His beard tickles. I could endure this form of torture for the rest of my life.

This man is perfect.

At first, our movements are slow, allowing me to adjust to his size. Then my fingers grip his hair as I plead, "More." And my man does not disappoint.

Angling his hips ever so slightly, his cock hits differently. Tickling me even more while also feeling like he is reaching areas never explored. My right leg begins to twitch uncontrollably, like I'm a dog humping its toy. I'm not sure what's coming over me, other than his cock.

"You like that?" he teases, smirking, knowing exactly what he's doing to me.

Securing myself tighter to him, I pant as sweat beads on my face. "Don't you ever stop."

Gabriel nips at my lips. "I wouldn't. Not even if you begged."

Loud moans leave me as his cock continues to impale me. My orgasm breaks through me. I am lost in a daze of bliss. Almost like I'm floating. Which is also very possible, considering he's a ghost. But reality quickly crashes down around me as my mind sobers. Because mid-bliss, I utter words I can never unsay and immediately regret as they leave my mouth. "Aye, aye, Captain Hook."

I freeze. All joy is sucked out of me and is quickly replaced by a distinct feeling of humiliation.

Thus concluding my grand return to sex.

And welcoming the start of a lifelong celibacy.

14. HARPER

Sitting in Fallon's library, I made an excuse to come over. I told her I needed to borrow a book for my upcoming ceremony. But really, I need to drop a truth bomb on her. Before coming over, I made sure the coast was clear. I knew Hails would be out back with her dad and Darla. And I know the timing of such truths is less than ideal, with the town opening tomorrow, but discussing the details of moaning *Aye, aye, Captain Hook* during the peak of my orgasmic bliss is top priority.

I'm sitting cross-legged on her dark green velvet couch, with a couple of random books piled in front of me I don't even need, waiting for Fallon to come in and check on me. Because she always checks on me;

she's a mom now, it's what she does and it's so freakin' adorable.

But my heart is racing. The anticipation could very well kill me. This is a lot of stress on this ol' chap. I've never been this tightly wound in all my twenty-odd years of life. The antique Victorian grandfather clock ticks loudly in the front entrance, taunting me. Could time move any slower?

Throwing my head back, it rests on the back of the couch while I drown in a river called self-pity. Aye, aye? What am I, a pirate?

"Everything okay?" Mom senses. A child in distress and she cannot help herself. My plan has worked perfectly. Lifting my head up, I turn to face her. Fallon's brow furrows in confusion as her eyes shift, looking me over. My face droops and confusion turns to worry as she waddles over. "Harper, talk to me. What's wrong?"

I don't answer her question. Instead, focusing on her beautiful baby bump. "You've dropped. It could happen anytime now." Fallon nods. Her facade lifts, and exhaustion is revealed. She still isn't sleeping. Dark bags hang under her tired eyes as she cradles her tummy. "It's the best and worst possible timing. I hope she holds out a few more weeks." Sitting next to me, she raises her bare feet on top of the coffee table. Her ankles are swollen, and her breasts are screaming *Welcome to Port Canyon!*

"I love you. You are so beautiful, Fallon." Her face falls, eyes welling with tears, while her lip quivers.

"I love you too, Harp-Harp."

And I instantly hate that I have activated her hormones, so I take the dive and blurt it out. "I said 'Aye, aye, Captain Hook' during sex last night."

Fallon's face transforms from an overwhelming emotional breakdown to an expression that I am unsure of. It sort of looks like she is trying to contain a fart. And just as I am about to reassure her that she can let it free, she busts a gut, laughing. "When did you have sex?"

I'm sorry. What?

"I'm going to pretend you didn't say that and continue with my story." Fallon immediately feels bad. Her face flushes and I feel she's about to say something more, but I stop her. "It wasn't anything. Until it was. Everything happened so quickly. I barely had time to process it myself, never mind tell you. I'm sorry. Please don't hate me."

Her hand slaps my knee playfully as her body wiggles in excitement. "Promise I won't hate you if you tell me everything. Right now."

Closing my eyes, because I am terrified of her reaction, I brace myself for impact as the words leave my lips. "I too have been dicked down by a ghost." Silence follows. I take it as my cue to continue. "Gabriel Knight's penis may have accidentally slid into my vagina... and my mouth. And I may have liked it so much, that I said 'Aye, aye, Captain Hook' while my leg shook viciously during the orgasmic bliss he gave me."

Swallowing, my throat bobs, feeling as dry as the desert while waiting for Fallon to respond. I peek through one eye to find her head is tilted and her arms are crossed over her chest. *Come on, Harper, woman up, take it on the chin.*

Opening both eyes. I look back at her, sitting in silence, waiting for her response. Fallon's mouth opens, then closes. I wince.

"Does his penis have a hook, or is it how he hits it?"

Her question catches me off guard, causing me to stumble over my words. That's what she took away from this?

"It's how... it's definitely how he hits it. My leg twitched like I was in heat." Her stomach bounces as tiny wheezing giggles start to reveal themselves. I can't believe how much she's enjoying this.

The heels of her feet kick against the hard coffee

table as her laughing fit continues. And in between the laughter and belly bouncing, Fallon manages to get a few words out. "Merrick's dad. Oh god, this is amazing."

Mumbling under my breath, I reply, "Yeah. Peachy."

Raising her hands, she waves me off, trying to calm herself. Sweat beads on my forehead and my palms dampen from the stress. And after taking a couple of deep breaths, Fallon is able to regain her composure. "I'm happy for you, Harp-Harp. I am, truly. This is so exciting, and I want to hear more about how it all started. I'm also very mad at you for keeping this gem from me for so long. But this, alongside Mark and Darla, you can't write this shit." She winks at me. "And he thought two girls were his karma. You're our new mother-in-law." Another wheeze follows. This girl is out of hand. And I can't help but join in.

She's right. About all of it. And I am totally here for it.

"If you aren't careful, you will either piss yourself again or give birth right here," I remind her between giggles, resting the side of my face against the couch. Fallon wipes her tears away, and that's when I notice through her thin white-and-black-striped shirt that she has lactated. Two large wet spots have formed around each nipple. This sends us into a delirious tailspin once I point it out. "You need to get better control over your bodily fluids."

And her response sends me over the edge. "I may as well pee myself, make it a trifecta." I love her.

Then, the sound of the back door opening causes both of us to freeze. Our eyes lock and we know who's coming. The sound of tiny feet follows. I panic, knowing I cannot keep a straight face around him. And I am not ready to break Merrick, only to then be broken by him in return. That asshole will haunt me into my next life and love it. I'm not built for that.

My head spins toward Fallon, who's already kicking her feet again in a fit of laughter. Bitch. She's my best friend, so I can call her that. Calm your tits. This is a very serious situation. We don't have time for this! The enemy is nearing.

Stumbling to get up, I finally jump to my feet and flee the scene, only causing her to howl louder. I swear evil still lives in this house. Traitor.

Finding refuge in my back garden, my fingers brush gently along the blooming roses and black lilies. It's early morning, and I have avoided the Knight household like the plague. While also avoiding my own family. The town opened yesterday, so this place is crawling with people. And Merrick's mission this year? Scare the shit out of this one guy who refuses to be scared. And I've never been so supportive of his destruction in my life, but desperate times call for desperate measures.

It doesn't explain why I've avoided Dad. Perhaps the fresh air can bring some perspective, help guide me to where I need to go when it comes to him.

Bees from the hives start to awaken, and I watch as a couple land on the flowers surrounding me. Watching them, and the rest of nature, calms me, soothes the soul and resets my mind. Dusk and dawn are my favorite times of day to sit and just be out here.

Ducking under a weeping willow, I rest my back against its trunk and slide down to rest. A small creek runs a few feet away, adding to the aura. Fog lifts from the chilled autumn ground and hovers over the open creek. The slight crisp chill provides comfort. This is absolutely the best time of year.

Fluttering eyes close, and as I am drifting off, I can faintly hear footsteps walking through the tall grass. Immediately, I know it's not Gabriel. He would just pop up, not walk. If it were Merrick, he would make himself known, and again, like his father, he would just pop up and surprise me. Fallon's too pregnant to waddle this far, thus leaving one possibility. My dad.

Clearing his throat loudly, I ignore the sound. He followed me to corner me. Knowing I couldn't possibly escape this conversation. Well played, Dad, well fucking played.

"Haven't seen you in a while, kid. What's going on?"

Arching my brow, I bite my lip feeling guilty, but keep my eyes closed. Shrugging, I respond, "I've just been busy with the town opening, I suppose."

Dad tsks at my excuse, seeing through me the second the words left my mouth. "You seem different. I'm your father. I notice these things."

My head tilts. What he is talking about and what I expected to be discussed are two vastly different things right now. Where is he going with this?

"I heard noises coming from your room a few nights back..." Opening my eyes in horror, my dad stands in front of me, scratching the back of his neck, equally uncomfortably. No, that's not possible because he heard me having sex. I am mortified. "I just hope you are being safe."

I stand, throwing my arms out. This conversation must pivot before I die of embarrassment.

"Nope. We aren't having this chat, Dad."

Relief washes over him, and his shoulders relax. "Thank you. But, please, maybe keep it down the next time your friend is over?" I stare back at him, still humiliated. And slightly pissed off. The audacity of him to ask this of me, when he can be heard two floors up fucking my dead mother. I take this opportunity to direct the conversation off me and on to him.

Daddy-O, it's time to be held accountable.

"Is this really why you came all the way out here? Be real, please, for once in your life, Dad." He's taken aback by my boldness. I am normally timid, compliant, and 'Harper' bubbly. But not today. Today I am Harper on a mission.

"I'm not sure what you are trying to get at here..."

Rolling my eyes at his response, the gates have opened and a flood is coming.

"Don't you think it's a little late to start acting like you give a shit? The sex talk is one you have with your kid in their teens, if not earlier. Not when they are in their twenties." Pausing, I allow my words to marinate before adding, "And don't worry, Mom gave me the talk before she died. Before I found her body contorted at the bottom of the stairs. In our home. In the very home where you refuse to ever address her death. As if magically it never happened and she's still alive and well."

Dad's face burns red, nostrils flaring while his fist clenches. I've obviously hit a nerve.

"You will not disrespect me in my home."

Waving him off, I ignore his command and continue my monologue. "I miss her every single day. Her smell. Her soft voice and warm presence. She was nurturing me to be the best version of myself. And when she died, I crawled into myself wanting to hide away from the world. I was so mad. I was so fucking sad."

My lips quiver. An ugly cry is slowly creeping up, and I'm not sure how much longer I can keep it at bay. The adrenaline that fueled this boldness is now wearing thin. If I'm going to hit this home, I have to move quickly.

"What you are doing with her will never bring her back to us!"

Dad's head falls back, attempting to mask his own grief from me.

"Be real. Show me you're sad. Tell me you miss her. Instead of preserving her in the goddamn morgue, in our family home, for you to fuck whenever you want. She deserves more than that. Give her, her dignity back. Give us peace, dammit."

My vision sees stars. The rush is blinding as my hands tremble. Dad spins, leaving his back to face me.

Coward. But I refuse to comfort him. He needs to hear this. Totally unfiltered and raw.

"You saved her from Joanie. That woman was a wicked cunt. But she's gone now. So, please, save yourself from this unbearable grief and guilt that you've been carrying."

Lowering his head into his hands, Dad's shoulders shake. He's crying.

I soften my tone, lowering my voice. I make a final plea. "Free her. Free yourself. Free us. Please." Pausing once more, I allow the words to sink in further. "You haven't even talked me through what will happen this month, at the full moon, when I assume responsibility for the morgue. Do you even realize that? You may not be a miserable old wench, but you are so fucking selfish, just like Joanie."

Dad wails into the morning sky. A flock of birds, disturbed by our hostile presence, flies out of the trees. And Dad walks away, leaving me alone from his path of self-destruction, again, to process. I don't hate him. I truly don't believe he knows any better, but I am furious and really, really sad.

Screaming into the heavens, I let out years of pent-up frustration and grief. More animals rustle in the grass, fleeing from around me. Holding my arms out wide, mist falls around me, eventually soaking my clothes and dampening my hair, and I feel liberated. Free.

Closing my eyes, I keep screaming and spin around in place. To get everything off my chest has lifted a massive, suppressed weight off me, and I am so damn proud of myself. As I stop. I peek my eyes open and see the rays of sunshine attempting to penetrate through the low Washington state clouds. The green grass glistens with droplets of moisture sitting on the blades.

"I am so proud of you, beauty."

Gabriel.

Spinning around on the balls of my feet, his hands stop me, gripping my shoulders. His smile stops my heart. A cheeky wink ignites it into a rapid beat.

"Good girls deserve to be rewarded."

I tilt my head, curious. Something twinkles in his eye and I step forward, still feeling the rush. My chest rubs against his spectacular pectorals, and I whisper against his bare neck, "Then show me."

Before I can step back, he hoists me up just to lower me down gently. A tiny *yip* escapes me from being surprised.

Lying on the damp grass, I let my head fall back and my body rest while waiting to see what is coming next. Then I notice Gabriel is dry. His luscious mane is not at all affected by the light rain. Perks of being a ghost, I suppose, and completely unfair. Once this rush wears off, I am going to be positively miserable and cold.

"Let's see how long I can keep your sweetness on my beard. I hope long enough for a midnight snack. If not, I will just have to come back for seconds."

My body melts into the earth. He's going to test out his flavor savor on me. And I am as giddy as I was the first day I forced my friendship on Fallon. My pussy aches, and I don't know if my panties are soaked from being legitimately wet or from being horny. Let's be honest, it's definitely both now. Gabriel swiftly removes my skintight leggings from my body and another mortifying moment is about to occur between us. I am in my 'it's laundry day' granny panties. Nothing about my current predicament is sexy. Covering my face in embarrassment, yet again, I wish for him to go away and leave me to wallow half naked on the ground in peace.

Instead, he speaks while tickling my lady bits over my cream-colored, full-coverage, and saggy panties. "My, my, what do we have here?" I cringe. *Please make it stop.* "Did you wear these sexy panties just for me?"

I can't bear to open my eyes to witness his mocking expression. His fingers stop teasing, and I am relieved. And just as I am about to peek through my fingers, I am met with a suction cup on my vagina. Gabriel is giving me head through my grandmother's panties. His hand pushes up my stomach, searching for the hem that will never be found, because it is comfortability resting under my boobs.

His hot breath warms me while he stops his sexual and consenting assault on my lady bits. "I'm not even taking the piss. You need to buy more of these. They are doing things to this man that can only be described as wicked." Then, in one swift movement, he flips me over. I'm lying on my stomach, my face pressed against the wet earth, as he props my hips up, leaving my ass in the air. The damp crotch sags down. I wiggle my hips quickly and feel it swaying about, only to feel a sharp sting on my ass after.

"Stop moving. It's my playtime, not yours." His voice is stern, and I am very fucking aroused.

Unable to help myself, I respond sarcastically, "Sir, yes, sir." Which is only followed by another spank and his deep and delicious voice.

"Don't you mean, aye, aye, Captain Hook?" Oh, nope. I'm done. Absolutely not.

Attempting to get up and run far, far away. Gabriel's strong hands stop me, pushing down between my shoulder blades firmly and leaving me unable to move and stuck in this horrible state of existence. Yes, I am being dramatic, but this is all less than ideal right now.

"You are going to stay still and let me feast. Do you understand me, Harper?" He gives the illusion of this being a question, but it's a command, which I accept as long as I can keep my face buried in the dirt.

Gabriel bunches my panties together, gathering both sides and shimmying them into the middle of my butt crack, creating a sexy granny thong. Then, alarmingly, his nose follows the cotton-blend fabric. Once Gabriel is satisfied with the snug fit between my cheeks, his finger hooks into the sagging crotch, pulling it to the side and exposing me to all the wildlife I once called friends. They will never come near me again after seeing this.

My man starts slowly, with tender kisses against my throbbing lips. His trimmed beard tickles against my sensitive skin with each movement. The tip of his tongue follows, circling my entrance like a murder of crows getting ready to pounce on their prey. I relax into it, his hold, his tongue, and let the magic of this man take over.

My body squirms. Aching for added friction, but I have learned recently that good things come to those who wait. Moans and groans vibrate between my thighs as Gabriel toys and teases. Every so often he will suck on my clit, getting me just to the brink before pulling back and flicking the bean with his tongue. My hands flex, needing to grip on to something as my body yearns for its release. Gabriel's tongue laves me, drawing designs, as a loud growl from deep inside his throat escapes and gives me shivers. He devours me. My muscles contract, and I am on the brink. I'm not sure I can hold it back any longer, but I also never want him to stop. With one final move of his talented tongue, Gabriel sucks my pussy hard as I come into his mouth. He laps it up, sucking me harder, needing every drop I can give. My leg twitches and I fight all urges to call him captain.

Then, as I am trying to distract myself from opening my mouth, like a cold bucket of water being dumped over me, I realize what he's spelling out with his tongue as he sends me into an orgasm coma. *Love.* And all in lower case to get that figure eight motion.

Collapsing once he releases me, my brain is dazed, and I am unable to move. Aftershocks ripple through me, causing my legs to vibrate with each one. Another playful spank follows against my bare bottom this time, only adding to the afterglow. I'll deal with the L-word later, and until then I will bask in this glory.

The world quiets. It's only the two of us that matter in this moment. And just as I think he will lay next to me, soft words are spoken in my ear. "I'm so proud of you."

Rolling my head over, Gabriel's blue eyes look back at me. His body is floating just above the damp ground as I admire my cum, which is sticking and glistening on his beard. I want to get emotional. His words mean the world to me. I feel them deeply because I know he truly means them. But I can't, because today has already been very draining.

Instead, I confess, "These are my grandmother's actual panties."

15. Darla

That umbilical grandson of mine still hasn't realized his brother is fucking me. And I like it. It's comical. What isn't, is seeing our sweet Harper moping.

"What do I do?" Tears stream down our sweet girl's pale cheeks. Sadness encompasses her. And my heart breaks. Doug, her father, is a piece of work, but I know they will get through this.

Wrapping my arms around Harper's shoulders, I squeeze her as tight as I can, allowing her to rest and lean on me as I try to lift some of the burden off her. "Your dad will come around. You were brave to speak your truth to him. Harper Hayes, you have come a long way from the first time I met you. No longer timid, shy, and masking your trauma behind your bubbly personality. You are finding yourself, and I am forever proud of you."

Instead of further relaxing into my embrace as we sit secluded in the graveyard, her body tenses.

Confused, I ask. "Sweet girl, tell me, what's wrong?"

Soft words follow as her eyes squint and head cocks sideways to look at me. "No, Darla, he loves me."

I am quick to respond. "As he should. He's your father. He may not show it as well as others, but of course he loves you."

Harper's eyes shift, brows raised in shock now as her head shakes. "No. Gabriel."

If I had saliva, I would be choking on it right now. Or if Mark's cock was in my mouth. That man is talented.

I'm glad that's cleared up. This conversation could have gone completely sideways otherwise. Clearing my throat, I squeeze her again, trying to show no judgement, only love and comfort. "And did you say it back?" I pry, genuinely curious.

Harper shakes her head no. "He spelt it on my vagina while sucking cum out of me. I moaned instead. What if he's changed his mind? Or he's mad at me? I've never had this before. I don't know what I'm supposed to do."

Letting go of her, I move to face her head-on. This talk just took our relationship to a new level and I need her to hear me when I say this. Centering myself so I am looking her dead in the eye, I tell her the truth. "You love him."

Harper's face contorts into a look of extreme horror. How dare I suggest a thing. I go on to explain my statement. "You care about him enough to worry. From what I have gathered, you feel confident enough in the situationship to tell your best friend about it. You came seeking him just the other day. You. Love. Him." And I rest my case.

Pulling back, her eyes look up and down my body, as if I am speaking another language and she is wildly confused by it all. Pishposh.

"Was he mad after? Gabriel is a grown-ass man. He would tell you if he were upset. He told you about Joanie, so why hold back if he was upset?" Harper's face falls, knowing I have a point.

"No, he told me..." Her eyes drop to the ground, ashamed, as she continues. "He told me he was proud of me." Tears well in her eyes, but she waves it off, not wanting to draw attention to them.

"He has been watching you since you were seventeen. You are only joining the party, and he knows that. That man will wait a million lifetimes to have you.

And three words not being said back, yet, will not turn him away. He will wait because he loves you."

Harper nods as the words sink in. I only speak the truth.

Before allowing the silence of the night to fall around us. I reiterate, "You love him." Pausing, I need to choose my next words carefully, because I love my granddaughter Fallon endlessly. We all do. I know she supports her best friend, but her baby daddy can be rather moronic. And so can Harper's selfish father, Doug. "Screw the haters. They either accept you, and who you love, or they can bend over and let me shove something hard up their asses aggressively."

Soft laughs follow as her shoulders bounce and a smile forms across her face, wiping away the evidence of any sadness. Clasping my hands together, I wouldn't be a good grandmother of sorts if I didn't say this last bit. "Never allow anyone to dim your happiness."

Naturally, Harper rolls her pretty slate eyes at me. "Darla, I'm an overthinker."

I cannot argue with that. But that's what makes our girl so special.

"But speaking of your father. A little birdie told me..." Harper leans forward, invested. "He has requested a plot. So, whatever you said, or didn't say, to make Gabriel praise you like he did. Well, it seems like it may have worked." I am always up for a little girl-time gossip.

Harper's jaw nearly drops to the ground, eyes wide, shock riddling her. "Keep talking to him. You are the nudge he needs. Avoidance is no longer working. Holding him accountable is. You have grown so much, sweet girl." I add, "This goes for Gabriel too. Talk to the boy. It may surprise you." I smirk, knowing I'm right. Because I'm always right.

"I'm not ready for my ceremony. He hasn't prepared me. I feel more helpless going into it than Fallon did."

And here comes the blunt aspect of our relationship. "You know exactly what to expect. What will happen and when. You are the one who guided Fallon, pushed her to find the truths behind our town, or have you forgotten?" Harper is taken aback, but I don't care. "You will go into your mother's closet. I know your dad hasn't packed it away, and you will find your dress there. The goblet and blade are where they always have been.

"On the upcoming full moon, we will gather. You will recite the same words Fallon did, and the town will pass the legacy on to you. Forever tying you to Port Canyon, just as we have done it for centuries."

Harper rolls her eyes at me once more, knowing

I'm right. She's nervous, and needs a bit of handholding, but if she expects it from her father, it will only continue to bring her disappointment, until he has dealt with his own issues. But I know she will be fine. Harper was made for this life. She takes pride in this town and her role. I'm not worried. If there was any doubt, I would force my involvement more, but this is simply cold feet. I just hope no one levitates then passes out for days at this one. I cannot take another Knight boy being overbearing and nitpicking. It did my head in during the last one.

Her features soften as she rises to her feet, brushing any loose debris off her bottom. "Thank you for always being here when I need you." Pulling her in close, I squeeze her once more before letting her go. "You are so strong. And so very loved. And if anyone tries to harm you, I will fuck them up." My last comment makes her laugh. But it's true, I would cut a bitch for every one of my people.

Our warm embrace ends, and Harper smiles at me once more before turning to leave through the thick foliage. And just before she is out of sight, Mark pops up, startling me. I scream and Harper turns around in a panic. I slap his arm playfully as I scold him. "Don't do that." But his face doesn't relax. Panic envelops him. "He knows." And now it's my turn to be confused.

Mark continues when I don't respond. "Merrick knows. He saw us by his tree. He fucking knows."

Smiling, I'm excited. Because I'm not afraid of that ghost.

16. Gabriel

"Hello?" Mark's voice echoes in the yard. I asked Darla to send him over, but to be vague in all details. And like a boy addicted to pussy, he listened.

"Over here," I shout from under the garden gazebo. This one is more secluded than the others. Made of gray stone, pillars surround me with a domed roof overhead. Tiled with black-and-white marble, green vines provide a beautiful contrast. Sweet songs of baby birds chirping provide an added ambience as Mark cautiously walks up the stone path toward me.

Dark hair covers his forehead, deep wrinkles trying to peek through as he looks around. Hands are secured in his front pockets, and his body is tense at the shoulders. "Fuuuck," I can hear faintly coming from his lips.

And awkwardly, I raise my hand and wave. Mark's head shakes in disbelief. He doesn't return the greeting.

"Who else knows?" is his first question as he steps into the gazebo. And it's fair. Anything he has to say, or feels, is completely valid, and I am ready for it. "Just you, Darla, Fallon, and Harper." He nods in understanding.

"Why?" My head cocks in confusion, unsure of which 'why' he is referring too. His eyes take me in while standing at the entrance. "Why now?" My brows scrunch together and my eyes drift to my feet.

"That isn't my story to tell. But I am here to stay, if that's okay with you, son?" I feel great shame. Abandoning my boys all those years ago. It was wrong, but I can't take it back. I can only do better from here on out, if they allow me.

"Merrick can be rather dramatic, can't he? Easing into it with me was the smart move, old man," Mark jokes. Glancing up, I am welcomed by a crooked smile on his face, and my body relaxes. This is the step in the right direction. I can't wait to reconnect with my boys.

Holding my hands out, I offer him a seat on the stone bench as I sit down, crossing my feet at the ankles. Mark casually walks over, taking a seat next to me. Hunched over, I turn my head and take him in again. He's a man. With a kid. And dead too soon. "The curse got you?"

Raising his brows, Mark's quick to respond. "Appears so. Just when I thought I beat it, she fucking took me."

Nervously, I comb my fingers through my hair. "So, you and Darla?" His shoulders shrug, unashamed. "Who knew?"

I throw my head back, laughing. "Who fucking knew, indeed. You don't understand just how relatable those two words really are, son."

My kid's hand pats my back. "Oh, but I do."

Shit.

"We don't keep secrets. But don't worry, I haven't said a word," he reassures me before asking his original question once more. "Why now?"

Clearing my throat, I press my lips together, trying to find the perfect words to answer with. "She needed to be seen. Was silently begging for anyone to notice. Desperate. And I *needed* her to know she was." I pause briefly, still gathering my thoughts. "I checked in on you boys from time to time. It was too painful to stay for too long. And putting my feelings ahead of yours was wrong. I thought I was saving you from the same ending as me if I just stayed away. I should have done more, done better. Because she ended up killing us all anyway. I'm sorry."

Tears well in my son's eyes. "We were so angry at you. It's why I tempted fate and fled. But I wouldn't change it. Everything that happened, good or bad, gave me Fallon. My light. My pride and joy. And now my grandbabies. I was very angry, but I'm not anymore. None of us could have predicted our own outcomes. Merrick died because he is dramatic and hated *her* more than you. My ultimate demise was the curse. So I guess it was kind of predictable. It had the element of surprise along with it, never knowing when it may strike me down. But thank you for apologizing, Pops... Thank you."

Gripping his knee, I give him a tight squeeze.

Lightening the mood, Mark throws me a curveball. "I heard you spelt love while giving head."

If I had water in my mouth, I would have spat it out immediately from shock.

Then, in unison, we say one name, "Darla," and laugh.

"Yeah. And I will tell her in as many ways, and as many times as it takes for her to believe me. And once she does, I will keep going."

"You've always been this way, Pops. A romantic.

Joanie could never appreciate you enough for it. She never understood how lucky she was to have you and us. But Harper will. She's been an invaluable friend to Fallon. Her heart is barricaded. It takes good energy and proven trust to get past it, but if anyone can break those walls down, it's you."

I squeeze him once more in appreciation. I don't deserve such kindness from him this soon, but he's giving it and it's touching areas inside me I forgot existed.

"I will ease her into us for as long as it takes. Until the end of time, son. If it means I can be with her." Pictures of Harper flash in my vision, laid out beneath me, shy and blushing.

Mark speaks up, visions of my beauty fading. "What now?"

Clasping my hands together, that is a great question. And I am not entirely sure of what the right answer is.

"Harper's ceremony is in a few days. We all should be there for her during it. I'll stay hidden. That night is all about her and I refuse to take that away. Then, who knows?" What will be, will be. I'm trying not to force anything with this second chance of happiness. I only want to do what feels right. And she is what's right.

"Have you thought about telling Merrick? Or when you will?" His follow-up questions are ones I'm not sure of. It will never be the 'right time' when it comes to my oldest. Regardless, his processing will be the most unique and unhinged. Perhaps you could describe him as volatile.

"You know what, kid? I have no idea. It will be a last-minute, spur-of-the-moment thing, I suspect."

Tiny footsteps distract us both. Harper knows I'm out here. I told her about seeing Mark and she was anxious enough for the two of us about it.

"Well, Pops. I will leave you to it. Don't be a stranger. It's been nice seeing you again." Mark stands up, and I follow his lead. Reaching my arms out, I pull him in for a warm embrace and he returns it.

"I've missed you so much, kid." Emotion tries to creep up my throat, but I push it back down.

He murmurs, returning the sentiment, "Me too, Pops. Me too."

I sense Harper watching us as we break apart. Cheerfully, she greets us. "Hello, boys. And how are we?" She raises her brows in anticipation.

"If we thought Merrick had lost his mind over Darla and me, I cannot wait to see his reaction when he finds out about you two." Mark throws his head back in hysterics, while sneaking by Harper, leaving the two of us alone. What a dick. I join him, chuckling. He isn't wrong, though.

Her arms cross, face stern, and I would melt into her if I could. She is so fucking cute right now. I walk up to her, cupping her face with my hands. "How's my beauty?"

Harper's body transforms from the question, slumping into me. "He agreed. We will bury her tomorrow."

I wrap my arms around her, squeezing her tight, letting her know I am here, always. We stand here, embracing one another in silence, until she breaks it. "I thought I would be excited. Relieved, maybe? But it's like she's died all over again. And tomorrow could be my final good night to her. We can hope she comes back as a spirit, like you did. But nothing is guaranteed and..." I don't push, I wait, comforting her by rubbing circles on her back. Emotion riddles her voice as she continues. "This could be the last time I see her. And I'm going to miss her so much."

Harper's body shakes against mine. "I will do everything I can to make sure this isn't the last time. I promise, baby."

She wipes her nose on my shirt, sniffling. "I know."

Her head rises, those beautiful blue slate eyes meeting mine. Her face is cute, red, and blotchy from crying, and saliva sticks to her lips as she speaks. "Thank you."

Pressing my lips firmly against her sweet forehead, I reassure her, "Always. I got you, always."

17. Harper

It's midnight.

The ocean tides are high. The lunar cycle is in full effect as the crescent moon shows us just a sliver of herself in the night sky. A warm breeze dances through us as nature embraces our energies and comforts us. We gather here to grieve, to close a chapter before a new one opens in mere weeks.

I spent the day with Mom, washing her one last time. Perhaps our last intimate moments together. Her makeup is elegant, a touch of mascara and a nude brown shadow on her lid with a black wing. Red decorates her lips, and the touch of fair bronzer on her cheeks and forehead make her glow. Mom's long hair rests on her shoulders, and a silver pendant from Dad, engraved, sits around her neck. The finishing touches were a beautiful yellow summer dress, no shoes, just how she liked it, and a couple of flowers from the garden laying with her.

Dad is somber. He had his final moments with Mom last night before allowing me to take care of her. Numbness may riddle him now, but feelings will rise to the surface, eventually, and he will have to deal with them. There will be no running from grief, because it will always catch up to a person. Haunt them in dreams and pictures. And once he accepts that, works through it all, we will be able to move forward, as a family. This step forward gives me great joy in a time of sadness, and it's nice seeing a light shining through the darkness, finally.

A couple of local boys Fallon hired for the month, as extra help, carry Mom through the graveyard. We pass the angel of death, and I bow my head to her in respect and gratitude. Thanking her for watching over all the souls which live here. Tiny lights line the walkway as we follow the casket, and behind me and Dad are Fallon, Merrick, Mark, and Darla. And I know, because I can feel him. Gabriel is watching over us as well.

Wearing a long black lace dress, with a black slip underneath, it's nothing fancy. It flows past my feet, so like Mom, I am barefoot. If I wasn't, there is a great possibility that I would have tripped and eaten the same dirt she's being buried in. Dad is in black slacks, dress shoes, and a charcoal polo shirt. Hands are fisted in his trouser pockets. I see them bulging out on either side of him. If he's angry, I accept it and will take it head-on. I know in my heart of hearts this is what's right.

As we get closer to Mom's plot, a tall pile of dirt comes into view. Her headstone is not yet finished, but we kept is simple in hopes we won't have to visit it for long. We hope she transitions over like Gabriel did. But Dad pumped her full of embalming... I shake my head, ridding my thoughts of the lingering doubt. I need to believe this will work.

Leaving the path, the bottoms of my feet crunch against the grass and dried leaves that have fallen from the trees. Crickets chirp, singing, which provides us with music as lightning bugs flutter around. The procession stops. Mom's casket is placed on the manual lift that, once we have said our final words, will lower her to rest.

Fallon interlaces her fingers with mine, a silent sign of support and love. She's my rock, my person. Merrick lights his joint. The smell of weed lingers under our noses. Dad sniffs loudly. He either is trying to get high or is alarmed by how rancid it smells and is turning his nose up. Considering his state, I go with option one. Anything to hide from reality.

Clearing my throat, I step forward. My hand squeezes Fallon's once before releasing her. My focus is on Mom as I allow words to flow freely from within, unfiltered and unapologetically.

"My hero. My first true love. My security blanket when I got scared, or shy, or nervous. The little nudge I always needed. You would see things I couldn't and encourage me to go in the right direction. And as time has passed, I believe this is still your work. Still you nudging and smirking from behind your hand as I discover what you have seen all along. I was so lost. Confused and angry. Too many scary thoughts that will shock them to hear. I masked it well. But you knew, even in another life, you guided me. I cherish our tiny moments together and our one-on-ones, but it never felt right. You were never meant to have an afterlife in our morgue. We both know he meant well, but Dad without you is lost. And I think it's time you nudged him more, guided him and reminded him that not all is lost, because I am still here. We are still here. I feel you in everything I do lately. Your spirit may not be in its physical form yet. Fingers crossed. But your energy lives within me every single day. I love you, Mom."

I don't cry. It alarms me at first, but then I notice I feel immensely lighter. A burden, a weight, a resentment has been lifted. Looking behind me, I find Dad looking back. Tears fall down his cheeks as his body vibrates. He's uncomfortable, he's sad, he is growing. This will help him, change him for the better. In time, he will see that too.

"Daddy?" His head shakes. "I've said what I have needed to up in here, sweetie." Pulling one hand out of his pocket, he taps his temple repeatedly as his bottom lip quivers. I nod in understanding. I've pushed him enough with this. He has been punished enough.

White roses from the garden sit, resting where her tombstone will stand. Stepping forward, I take one in my hand, kiss the thin skin-like petal with its tiny veins running through it. My nose inhales its beautiful sweet and warm scent, before tossing it on top of her final resting place. The rest follow, making the same gesture as the boys begin to crank the lift, lowering Mom down into the ground.

Stepping back, I walk to the other side and take a handful of dirt. As I wait for Mom to be completely lowered, my gaze wanders as the branches of the trees rustle. Another warm wind breezes by and I take a deep breath in. Stars sparkle, twinkling brightly in the night sky. And I can't help myself. I smile.

It takes several minutes for the boys to finish, but I am in no rush. I'm actually shocked Merrick hasn't said anything all night. Looking over to Fallon, I wink in appreciation and she knows exactly what it's for, giving a curt nod in return while rubbing her tummy. She's in pajamas, because she's pregnant and threatened my life as well if I made her squeeze her body into something uncomfortable. And I believe her. She could absolutely get away with murder right now. The woman is very hormonal. Nothing would stop her.

Taking my last step toward the open grave, I toss the handful of dirt on top of it and whisper, so only I can hear, "See you soon." And that concludes the burial.

Dad is the first to leave. His pain is running deep, but it will get easier with time. Darla and Mark follow suit. Merrick leans against a tree, a fresh joint hanging out of his mouth as he salutes me, then vanishes too.

Fallon goes to leave next, but I stop her. "I'll walk back with you." She tries to wave me off, but I ignore her, leaving the young boys to finish filling the plot back up.

Linking my arm through hers, we head back to the house, but something grabs my attention in the thick foliage around us. I look off, trying to find the source, when I catch a quick flash. It happens in the blink of an eye. Unless you were looking for it, you wouldn't see it.

It's Gabriel. He was here with us too, and emotion floods over me. I wipe my nose, trying to stifle my sniffles to not draw attention.

I adore that man.

18. Harper

"Harper. He is losing his mind. Ever since finding Darla and Mark together, he has been suspicious of everyone!" Fallon whisper-shouts through the phone.

I want to tap my fingers together and cackle like an evil mastermind, but you can tell it's driving her insane. This is her way of nudging me to reveal all, but I'm enjoying this too much. It's about time he felt what it's like being on the other side of things.

"Please, keep it between us just a little longer. I haven't even spoken to Gabriel about telling other people. Because, eventually, I know we will have to." In reality, I will drag this out for as long as I can. The most opportune time to reveal all has yet to show itself.

She groans from the other end of the line. Such a

hassle, I know. I roll my eyes, because she can't see me and I am an understanding, kind, and compassionate friend who will not argue with a pregnant lady.

"I should let you go. You need your rest, and I need to decompress from the day. It's been a lot these past few days."

Fallon yawns, and I follow suit.

"Thank you for letting me know you got home safe. Have fun masturbating. Night! Love you!"

I smile. This girl cannot be tamed. "Love you, too," I tell her back before reaching over to hang up the phone.

I'm laid out on my bed, still in my black dress, and with my limbs hanging out like a starfish. I reach for my pillow and smother myself screaming. Even if I didn't quiet myself, Dad wouldn't hear me, but better to play it safe. I don't need questions regarding my distress. When I got home, I called for him before trekking upstairs for the night. He didn't respond, but the door to the morgue was open. I stood at the opening for a few moments, but I couldn't hear anything. Giving him space, I let him be, to mourn, to say goodbye to the comfort of always having her around, because this is our new reality. And, if he were masturbating to the memory of her in that contraption he built to keep her preserved, I didn't want to walk in on it.

I've seen enough fucked-up shit to last a lifetime.

Cold hands find my ankles. And I continue my dramatics into my soft pillow. My body is flung about so I become centered on the bed, and my screams of sexual frustration stop. Slowly, the pillow is pulled away from my face. I loosen my grip on it, allowing him to take over. Wiggling my hips, I do a cute little shimmy and think it's my lucky day. Pound town, here I come.

Opening my eyes, the light is blinding. I cover my face with my hands to shelter myself from such a wicked assault. "Why are the lights on? It's nighttime." I pathetically sulk, because tonight, I am allowing myself to be exhausted and dramatic. And combining the two creates the version of me you're currently getting. You're welcome.

And remember, friends don't judge friends... to their faces. And right now I can see you, so be kind. I did just bury my mother, after all.

Now let me get back to my sexy ghost, who is likely going to manhandle me into a slippery mess of sexual bliss as he does that fun thing with his hips that makes it feel curved and dangerous.

"We aren't having sex." And just like that, he bursts my blissful bubble. Asshole.

Pouting with my bottom lip jutting out, I bat my sad eyes, hoping he will take pity on me, but he shakes his head, smiling. "This technique stopped working on me when my boys were little. Sorry, beauty. No sex tonight. Just love and cuddles."

Crossing my fatigued arms, I frown. "Lovemaking?"

Gabriel immediately busts a gut in laughter. I see nothing funny here. So, as a consolation prize, he pulls up my dress to reveal my lace panties, because it is no longer laundry day. Bending over, his lips meet mine through the lace, he kisses them gently, whispering, "Your mom is too exhausted to play tonight. She needs her rest. I'll be back in the morning, I promise." I giggle. He's always so sweet.

Sitting up, he lowers my dress back down and smiles at me. His eyes feel like they are penetrating my soul and my body warms. "I love that giggle." He speaks his words with lust, like he is hypnotized, only falling deeper into me the longer he stares. And, honestly, I am slightly uncomfortable. Not by him, but by it... what it is. I'm not sure what to do. It's like when someone hugs me, I'm never sure how long to hold them for, so I just squeeze until it's awkward and uncomfortable for both of us. Then I'm less lonely in the experience.

My eyes squint back at him when he doesn't move. "Whatcha doing?" His smile continues to illuminate the room alongside the lights. It's starting to get really fucking bright in here. Gabriel doesn't answer me. And I thought I was strange. This is just bizarre.

"Your strength this evening was inspiring. You were fearless. Holding the weight of your grieving father on your shoulders. And you did it with such confidence and elegance. The words spoken to your mother, while never losing hope and holding your dad accountable, respectfully. If I haven't said it enough, please let me know, because I am so proud of you."

My foot rises, creeping up the length of his jeans. Because I don't know what to say, I'm not used to this much attention. So, I am diverting it back to him. His hand grips my ankle, stopping me from moving any higher, sadly.

"Say 'thank you, Gabriel.' Take the compliment, beauty."

Then suddenly, I want to hide inside myself. "I'm grieving. You can't be calling me out like this." I can feel my cheeks warming, which means I am as red as a tomato. Releasing my foot, he cups my face. His thumb rubs my bottom lip.

"You never need to hide from me. I love and accept you as you are, Harper. And I will continue to compliment you until I am blue in the face. Because you are always worthy."

My throat tickles as I choke up. This asshole. He's so nice. And so understanding and considerate and...

"And we aren't having sex tonight because I will not take advantage of you in this condition."

Fuck, I was talking out loud. My hands cover my face, shooing him away, but he stops me, holding each wrist while placing my arms above my head.

"Tonight, let me compliment you, admire you, be proud of you, and hold you."

I nod my head in acceptance. Before he lets go of me, I close my eyes because they cannot be open for this next bit. "Darla seems to believe that I love you, too."

I expect a laugh, judgment, a look on his face that I can't stand. But since my eyes are closed, I cannot tell if that last part is happening.

Gabriel isn't laughing. He isn't saying anything.

My heart sinks into my stomach.

The dreaded rejection. It's a killer. Silent but deadly.

My body aches as he breaks contact with my skin. He's mad. Shit. Talking to Darla was a mistake. I knew it. Sharing details about us with her, I should have discussed this with him first. My mind races down the endless pit of voices, making me feel like shit. I love anxiety, don't you?

"Darla is never wrong." My eyes snap open. He spoke. He's still here. And he's absolutely right, she's a wizard of wisdom.

The tips of his sexy man fingers tickle the top of my forehead as they skim around my face. His eyes are soft on mine as I continue to blush, originally from embarrassment, but now from relief.

"I will always keep you safe, Harper. I am yours to keep, and I do not take that lightly. You have your pick of the litter, but you are choosing me. And it will be an honor and privilege to stand by your side."

His words instantly send my pussy into a tailspin of wetness.

My hand reaches for him, cupping his jaw, fingers toying with his trimmed beard. Our eye contact never breaks. "I love you."

The weight of his head rests in my hand. Eyelashes tickle his cheeks. "Please, never stop."

19. Gabriel

She's my favorite person.

My kids, by default, are a part of the same cluster. But I chose her, and she chose me back. Harper is gifting me a second chance of living, pun intended.

Her father, Doug, has been in the basement since last night. I checked on him while Harper was sleeping. She passed out shortly after tickling my nipples in an effort to have sex. It was a sad state of affairs from what I witnessed. I will say I am grateful Harper didn't have to see any of it.

Doug was standing in the temperature-controlled contraption his wife once lived in. Crying, with his head resting against the glass, while jerking off. I shed no judgment. Many of us have had grief-filled rub and tugs. And this is no different.

After rising for the day, Harper wasted no time jumping into the next task to tackle, preparing for her ceremony. I'm leaning in the entryway of her mother's grand closet. Staying hidden, I just stand and observe. Her long dark hair falls over her face as her eyes skim the many history books of Port Canyon surrounding her. All leather-bound, fragile parchment, discolored by age, and written in an inked quill pen.

She's nervous. Scared. Feeling alone and unprepared to take over the legacy that has been passed down from generation to generation in her family. The girl is in her head; she's her own worst enemy. Because she is the most prepared and qualified person for this role. She's been studying the legends and legacy her entire life because she genuinely loves what she does and couldn't wait for the day to come when it's fully hers.

A sigh of frustration follows. Her face is squished, like she's telling the page off in her head. It's so fucking cute.

Sneaking behind her, still out of sight, I move to her mom's jewelry case. An antique box standing on four gold legs. The base of the box is black, with gold trim and hinges. Delicate line designs in gold paint decorate the top. Gently gripping the lid, I will it open. Glancing behind me, I see if Harper has noticed, but her eyes are still on the books.

Beautiful emeralds and sapphires greet me. Her mother always had exquisite taste in fine jewels. But Harper isn't flashy, and on a night that will be all about her, to add to the attention would only cause her to crawl under her own skin further. Picking through each piece, I try to find one that matches her. Simple, stunning, quirky, and full of heart. And then I spot it. I hook the chain on my finger, holding it up. It's perfect. Gold chain links keep it together, not those tiny delicate ones but ones with some thickness to them. A gold clasp connects it together, with a yellow diamond in the shape of a heart sitting in the middle. It's everything Harper incorporated into this beautiful piece. And the yellow allows her mother to be close to her as she enters this next chapter. It also matches the dress Harper picked out for her mom to wear into the afterlife. The color holds a huge significance, and whether she sees it now or not, I'm unsure. But perhaps one day she will.

Turning around, Harper is still unaware of my presence. And if ghosts didn't roam your home, it would alarm you seeing jewelry floating toward you.

But thankfully, in Port Canyon, it's just another day in the life.

Kneeling behind her now, I bring the piece in front of her, and she startles. A gasp of fright follows with a hand to her heart. "Gabriel," she scolds, but I stay hidden. Because this is all about her, and I don't need the attention.

The yellow diamond twinkles and shines, the rays of sun lighting the closet from through the window capture its beauty perfectly. Gingerly, I place it around Harper's neck. It's snug, as I have now come to find. It's a choker that sits at her throat perfectly. Like it was made for her.

As the gold chain touches her skin, a shiver crawls up her spine. She swallows and her breathing becomes heavy. "I can't do this." I don't fight her on this. Instead, I stay quiet, allowing her to get the nerves out so we can pick out the perfect dress to match the perfect choker for the most perfect girl.

"I close my eyes to remember the passage I am to recite and with each try, I forget it. And the knife, what if it doesn't work and I am unable to collect the drops of blood from Dad? What if Dad doesn't show up because he is still reeling from Mom's burial? This entire thing could go up in flames, me included. I've never seen a failed ceremony before, but I assume the

Devil comes, ignites the land on fire out of sheer disappointment, taking the failure with him back to the dark depths of his lair."

Clasping the choker on, I can't help but show myself as I bust a gut. Between wheezes, I am able to get a few words out. "I don't think... The Devil?" I'm crying because I am laughing so hard.

Harper spins around on her bottom, arms crossed, face showing she is pissed. It doesn't help, only adding to my hysterics. "These are valid fears. You wait. You'll see. You won't be laughing as he takes me, kicking and screaming."

Holding my hand up, I try to compose myself long enough to respond with more than just a few words. My breathing begins to sound like a birthing technique. Wiping my tears away, I look her in the eye as seriously as I can muster, and tell her, "When did we bring the Devil into this?"

Harper's cute little fists pound the floor next to her. "Gabriel. These could be our last days." And now I have concluded, she's lost her fucking mind.

Continuing my birthing technique breathing, I inform her, "We have a treaty with the Devil. He won't be popping up here at any time, for any reason."

Harper's jaw drops in shock. And for you, the viewer, please note I am totally just fucking with her.

"Are you kidding me?" I shrug my shoulders casually, not breaking my composure. This is too good to stop. "You mean I could be why he violates it? Damning the entire town?"

Waving her off, I say, "Nah, I'm sure it will be fine. I wouldn't worry." I add a wink at the end, only to further freak her out.

If she were thinking rationally right now, she would realize that nowhere in our town's history books does it reference the fucking Devil or treaty. But she's actually lost her mind. Stress does wild things to a person, it seems.

My hands grip her shoulders. "Harper. I am screwing with you. None of that will happen. You will be amazing and if you forget something, we will be there to lift you up. Now, get out of that head of yours. It's not doing you any good." I reach up, tapping her temple gently. Harper's face falls. Exhaustion reveals itself. "I should have let you sleep longer this morning before eating my breakfast."

Playfully, she hits my shoulder and a smile quickly follows as the memory replays in her mind. "Don't you ever say something so silly again." We both laugh as I bring our foreheads together. Our lashes tickle and tangle as our noses touch.

"Now, close those books and let's pick you out something to wear. Would you like that, pretty girl?"

Harper's lips brush against mine. Her warm breath soothes me as her soft words are spoken. "Yes. As long as you help me."

"Always."

20. Harper
October 28 - Full Moon

The town is alive. Guests come from all over to visit us.

Our small shops are bustling. Tiny bells ding every time a door opens. Children run around carefree in the town's center. Parents follow behind, barely paying attention as they take Port Canyon in. The full moon overhead is rising in the night sky and in a couple of hours, my rite of passage will be complete. But first I stroll, taking in the beautiful evening surrounded by happiness and cheer, forgetting about nerves, if only for a few minutes.

Stopping in the middle of the cobblestone road, I stare up, captivated. The moon is the brightest I've seen in recent memory. It lights up the entire sky, allowing us to view the mountains perfectly. A dusting of snow covers their peaks, and peace is welcoming me into its aura. Because I can confidently say this for the first time in a very long time. I am happy.

I'm wearing a black sweat suit, white sneakers, and my hair down. My mother's choker remains secured around my neck. As folks pass me, I catch them staring and the attention of it makes me uncomfortable, but I will never take it off. It holds too much meaning now. And the sweat suit is meant to off balance the attention. But it doesn't appear to be working. For fuck's sake.

Loud chimes fill the center. Looking up at the large clock tower, I note the number of times the bell is ringing. And immediately I go over the list in my head: outfit picked, goblet and knife are with Darla, hair is done, makeup is only being put on because Fallon is making me. Actually, she will be over any minute now and will be probably annoyed when she finds me not there.

But that doesn't stop me from going through my mental list. Legs and armpits are shaved, but my dad is still held up in the basement, a minor important detail I hope can be sorted by someone other than me soon. Shoes. I'm wearing my black Converse. In case the Devil does appear, I need to be able to flee as quickly as possible. Gabriel has reassured me many times that it won't happen, but what does that old man know? Wait. That was mean. He's a sexy old man. Just call him Daddy. Ew, no. Don't. That sounded better in my head.

And on the ninth chime, I take a final look around. Everyone is so genuinely happy and completely oblivious to the events that will later occur. Guests know surface-level things, like the ghosts and curses, details of legacies not among them. A bike's bell dings, a teen shouts, "Watch out." I jump out of the way, nearly avoiding death. Kids can be so reckless.

"I'll send Merrick after you if you don't watch where you're going." The kid looks back, panicked, before crashing into a few garbage bins and flying over his bike handles. I giggle. Serves him right.

Shrugging my shoulders, I begin my journey home, skipping and humming. How interesting. Who knew a little innocent violence would make me so happy.

Fallon scolded me. Like, really scolded me. She even paced, then cried, and the entire performance ended with her hands waving in the air to really drive her point home. It would seem that skin prep before makeup is really important to her. I had no idea.

Washing my face with a bar of soap and then slapping some body lotion on it is an unacceptable practice, apparently. I have learned my lesson. Lecture has been noted and I immediately ordered new supplies while the town is still open for the next couple of days. Imagine if she found out on November first, she would have had a coronary.

She's left me alone now. I am standing, looking at myself in the mirror, and I look beautiful. A brown smoky eye really makes my eyes pop. A baby pink blush nicely complements it along with a nude pink lip. I may need to do this makeup thing more often. I feel really good as I take myself in. Before I am able to turn around to put my dress on, Gabriel pops in, arms wrapped around my naked waist. His forearms flex, and my kitty meows. Watching him in the mirror, he leans down. His lips trail along my exposed neck and work their way down to my shoulder. "Fucking magnificent."

My body melts into his hold. His body encompasses my petite frame, always protecting me. Sweet kisses follow and I feel high in the sky. With hooded eyes, I try to keep my composure, but my sexy man is making it incredibly difficult. "I thought I was supposed to be a good girl tonight?" I tease, smirking.

The vibration of his chuckle goes all the way to my pussy. She reacts, throbbing.

He tsks me, pinching my nipple, and my back arches with a groan. "Not fair."

And his voice is seductive. "Life isn't fair." I try to wiggle against his crotch, but he only tsks me once more. "It's time for you to get ready, sweet beauty. Everyone is waiting." And he ruins the moment with that one sentence.

"Promise me. Promise me I can do this." I need his reassurance. He is the only one who can keep my nerves at bay. His blue eyes look into mine through the mirror.

His face is serious, and he means each spoken word. "You are the only one who can do this."

A lump forms in my throat. Nerves are turning into emotions and his words only add to the chaos in my brain. But those words are what I need to hear, on repeat, the entire time.

"Baby, let's go get you dressed."

I nod, reaching my arms to his, and I squeeze him in return. "Thank you."

We stand in solitude for a moment. He waits for me to lead and once I do, Gabriel follows me from the bathroom to my bedroom. Hanging on the back of my bedroom door is the dress we picked from Mom's closet. It's cream in color, and the fabric is thin and flowy. Gabriel takes it off its hanger and holds it high above me, murmuring, "Arms up." I listen, holding them over my head as he slides it down over my exposed body.

I'm wearing my grandmother's panties in a matching cream cotton blend, and with the thin see-through fabric, it actually looks trendy. Who knew?

The neckline sits straight across my chest, and the sleeves end up starting just past the shoulders, giving it a milkmaid vibe, minus the cleavage. I'm going for a classy milkmaid look this evening. It pinches at the waist, then flows to my feet. A slit sits high up both thighs with my wavy hair flowing over my shoulders.

"You are perfect." Gabriel's sweet words make me blush as I turn around to face him.

Wrapping my arms around his neck, I stand on my tiptoes and kiss his lips. Pulling back slightly, I whisper, complimenting him in return, "So are you."

I feel like if he were alive, he would be blushing now too. Cute manly Gabriel with rosy cheeks. Just picturing it gets me horny. I think I may need a fan under this thing to keep my pussy from making a mess of it.

His hands squeeze my waist as he takes a step back, taking a bended knee. With my Converse in hand, he keeps a hold of them as I slide my feet into each one. I am about to bend over to tie them, but he stops me, lacing them for me and finishing it with a kiss on both my inner thighs.

Rising, he adjusts my choker, placing the yellow diamond back in the center. His focus is sharp, not stopping until it is sitting absolutely perfect. Once satisfied, Gabriel steps back, holding his hand out for me to take. And I do.

Looking down at me, he asks one question. "Are you ready?"

I have no idea how I am to answer it until I do. The answer even catches me off guard.

"Yes."

The cool breeze is a nice relief as my internal temperature is boiling from nerves. I feel my underboobs sweating, and I immediately worry about perspiration marks. I pray no one notices or takes any photos.

Gabriel leads us through the vast garden on my family's compound. The stone paths swirl and twirl until we reach the open field. The small creek runs through it with a few weeping willows that Fallon had her guys decorate using fairy lights. At least one hundred bouquets of fresh flowers stand in tall glass vases. They are a mix of white roses, black lilies, pink orchids, and yellow daffodils. Large white candles are lit, dripping wax, and tears try to well in my eyes, but I reject them because Fallon would be upset if I ruined my makeup.

Looking next to me, I want to ask Gabriel, *when did this all happen?* However, in the midst of my amazement, he vanished. Or maybe it was before then, I don't know. I was too engulfed in my own thoughts, and now people think I'm holding my one hand up for no reason at all. Because it is definitely not being held anymore.

Stepping forward, on my own, I am welcomed by familiar faces: Fallon, Merrick, Hails, Mark, and Darla. I search for my dad, but it isn't until Mark nods to the left that I find him wallowing against a tree. Also, here are the other town elders holding lit torches, as the ritual calls for.

Darla steps forward. Her presence is warm, as she declares it's time. "Come join us, Harper."

I nod once while my heart races. I am so nervous. But it's fine. I am fine. I was made for this. This is my destiny. A chapter I cannot wait to begin. I tell myself all of this to help ease my worried mind.

A circle forms. Dad steps forward, taking his spot next to the others, and the goblet and knife sit idle before us. Reaching down, I grip the knife handle into my hand. Glancing over at my dad, he holds his palm out. His blood is the offering. And my body takes over. It knows this ceremony inside and out, and I trust it to guide the rest of me.

"As the legacy and legends bind you here tonight, to your responsibility, we gather here to honor you, this journey, and as elders, grant permission. Tonight, Harper Hayes, you will become the legacy for the morticians. Your family name and blood bind you to it and the ceremony solidifies its hold." Darla allows a minute for her words to sink in before proceeding. "Please draw blood from your elder."

My hand shakes, I take a deep breath to calm myself. Stepping toward my dad, I peer over my shoulder and find the circle has closed behind me as hands are tightly clasped. Taking the tip of the sharp blade, I embed it into my father's palm. Slowly, I slide it diagonally. And following behind is dark crimson. Some drips down his hand and onto the luscious grass before us. Once sliced from thumb to wrist, I drop the knife at our feet. It bounces twice before settling. Looking my dad in the eye, he gives a curt nod. It's his blessing.

"Please fetch the goblet, Harper. Allow the blood of your elder to fill it. Nothing more, nothing less," Darla instructs. I oblige. Reaching for the cool metal next, I wrap my fingers around its stem and hold it under Dad's fist. He is squeezing it tight so more of his blood seeps out of the cut. None of this bothers me. I've grown up with blood and gore and dead bodies my entire life. But drinking blood is new to me.

Once the goblet is full, Dad releases his fist and joins hands to join the tightly closed circle. Darla speaks once more. "Now, repeat after me." I focus on my dad, keeping eye contact with him, as Darla recites our town's sacred words. "My legacy. My legend. My responsibility. I swear to protect the sacred space that our ancestors and fallen elders call home."

Nervous fingers play with the goblet stem, but my mind is clear and the words come out without a single hesitation. "My legacy. My legend. My responsibility. I swear to protect the sacred space that our ancestors and fallen elders call home."

Darla continues. "To be their caregiver and provide sanctuary. Port Canyon, forever their home and mine."

I have never spoken truer words. Ensuring the dignity of each body, each soul, is my passion. "To be their caregiver and provide sanctuary. Port Canyon, forever their home and mine."

Emotions suddenly rise as I promise my life to this town. It's unexpected but not unwelcomed. My lips quiver as Darla recites the last sentence. "'Til death and in the afterlife."

My heart would never let the bodies I touch down. I would never harm, only protect and preserve, until death and in the afterlife. I take the vow seriously and repeat after her with confidence and pride.

"'Til death and in the afterlife."

As I bring the goblet of blood to my lips, Darla calls out to all the elders. "May the elders bless this sacred ceremony. May they bless Harper and give her the strength to fulfil her responsibilities that the founding families have gifted her. Blood for blood."

The taste is horrendous, I don't know how Fallon did this. The iron-tasting substance coats my mouth and throat. I gag as I feel it slowly moving down my esophagus and weighing down my stomach. My face cringes, but I am a strong, independent woman. I will finish every drop, because I have to. My chest convulses, my body wants to throw up, but I keep it down. Just barely.

Dad's warm blood dribbles out the sides of my mouth as I lean back farther, taking larger gulps. Its warmth slowly runs down my chin and neck, but I look to the moon for strength. And it doesn't disappoint. It's electric. Energy courses through my body, infiltrating my veins. The energy comes from the ground below me, to the mountains surrounding me, and the trees protecting me. Nature blesses and supports me. Water from the creek rises then crashes down. My fingers tremble, dropping the empty goblet to the ground. Blood stains the front of my dress as butterflies of all colors and species surround me.

Placing a hand to my chest, my eyes close while my head falls back. And my body feels more connected to Port Canyon than ever. Forever my home. My legacy.

Pulling my head up, the butterflies continue to surround me, and I am also greeted by Gabriel. His hands cup my face. "I am so proud of you."

Our eyes connect. Love radiating from both of us, my body buzzes. "Thank you. I'm proud of me too."

"Congratulations, Harper. The ceremony is now complete." Darla's voice faintly rings in my ears.

But it's Merrick's who brings me back to reality. "If I could shit. I would have done it in my pants just now. What the fuck are you doing here?"

Oh shit.

But Gabriel doesn't break contact with me. Only giving a little wink before responding to his alarmed son. "That's no way to greet your old man."

Shifting my eyes over to Fallon, I see her step in, placing her hand on Merrick's chest to calm him as his head cocks sideways. He wastes no time lighting a joint and exhaling a cloud of smoke.

Fallon cuts in before he can speak. Her tone is calm, and he wouldn't dare argue with her. "This isn't the time. Please." Her look is stern.

And Hails, not knowing better, scolds," Daddy, no swearing in front of corpses!"

We all burst out laughing. Her timing couldn't be more perfect. And I decide to take this opportunity to mess with our sarcastic asshole ghost.

I grip Gabriel's wrists as I bring them down and away from my face, and I kiss the inside of his wrist, leaving a bloodied kiss mark behind. Releasing him, I spin toward Merrick, smirking as I walk in his direction. We are going to have so much fun together.

Leaning forward, I whisper into his ear, doing my best to fight back my giggles, but smile from ear to ear, "I'm your mommy now."

Harper
Epilogue

Naked, I am laid out on a bed of red rose petals. The room is dark, except for the white lit candles that surrounded me. I clench my thighs in anticipation. My man loves making all my dreams come true, and today is no exception.

The hinges on my bedroom door creak as it slowly opens. Two tall shadows elongate against the wall. I bite my lip in disbelief. I cannot believe this is actually going to happen. My mouth salivates, knowing those shadows are coming for me. And I am giddy with excitement.

My bedroom door clicks closed. Their feet pad against the floor. They separate, making their way around me. By the end, there is one on either side of me. Curious eyes glance up and I am greeted by two delectable faces. Biting my lower lip, I lay still in wait, yearning for what's to come next.

Gabriel clasps his hands together, and his lips part, revealing his teeth. His smile is sinister. My sexy man is completely naked, his cock, which is well fucking hung, bobs, dripping precum, and I resist the urge to take him in my mouth. Because tonight, they are in control. I am at their service, but it is all for me and about me.

Wandering eyes move up his fit-as-fuck body and land on his bulging biceps, then his immaculate pectorals. Gabriel catches me staring and begins flexing, only making me purr louder with need. Hair falls over his forehead, and he rakes it back with his hand so nothing blocks his view of me.

Glancing across the ceiling, my focus turns to the other figure in the room. For one night only. His bald head shines as the flames flickering light bounces off it. I wonder if he's clean shaven or adorning his classic stubble. Making my way down, I am pleasantly surprised. Classic stubble it is. The farther down my eyes travel, the more real this gets as his hairy chest is proudly on display. I can't wait to grip the coarse hair between my fingers. And like Gabriel, he is fully exposed. His pubes are shaven, including his balls. And with a quick swivel of his hips, his cock kicks up and starts propelling around. I am truly the luckiest girl in the world.

Tonight, I am being Eiffel-Towered by my man, my king, my Gabriel. And celebrity hottie Chris Meloni.

Both men extend an arm each, presenting their hands. Reaching up, I gracefully place mine into theirs as they help me rise to my feet. Once standing tall, they both release me and Gabriel steps in front of me. The tips of his fingers dance along my skin, something I have always found soothing. My body relaxes into him. Another set of hands joins his, except for these fingers trail along my spine. My body reacts of its own accord, arching into it as my breath hitches. Gabriel takes one more moment with me. Soft eyes greet mine and his question is simple, yet powerful. "Do you still want this?"

I become shy, nuzzling my face into him, nodding.

He tsks. "Words, beauty. I need your words."

My lips kiss his chest, followed by a little nibble, causing him to wince. I giggle, and respond, "Yes."

It's been predetermined. No other man will enter my pussy. That is my man's and only his. But my mouth is fair game tonight.

Chris grips my waist and spins me around. Gabriel's chest is now pressed tightly against my back.

Chris steps back, gripping his hard cock and giving it a couple tight squeezes. It captivates me.

Gabriel loosens his hold on me. It's quickly followed by a sharp sting on my bottom, causing me to lurch forward. He chuckles seductively and his voice is sultry. "Now, bend over, my beauty. It's time to play."

My hips hinge, my body bends forward, and I feel Gabriel teasing my pussy with his fingers. With doe eyes, I keep my gaze on Chris as my head slowly make's its way down his torso. The tip of my nose brushes against his lusciously hairy stomach. With each blink my lashes get tangled in his course hair while my heart goes pitter patter with excitement.

Thick dark curls tickle my chin; the man has a bush for days. As my lips move through it seductively slow. Parting my lips, I allow some to enter my mouth and my tongue twists around it. Chomping down with my white teeth still showing, I give his hair a slight tug causing Chris to hiss and wince. Gabriel spanks my bottom in return and I fucking love it. Pulling my face back, the curls slide out, and I move down again where Chris's bobbing cock greets me next. I lick my lips, because I am famished. Another spank follows on my bottom, and I groan from deep within my chest. Gabriel bends over, peppering soft, long kisses along my back. His hips grind against me, teasing and taunting. I wish he would just get inside of me.

"Patience. Now, hold on to Chris and put his cock in your mouth."

My body tingles. This is the thrill of a lifetime.

Obeying, I steady myself on to Chris and kiss his cock once, letting his precum stain my lips. Gabriel adjusts, lining himself up before slamming into my pussy. The invasion jolts me forward. My mouth opens and lips wrap around Chris.

Neither man takes it easy, thank goodness. I hate slow and boring things. I need commanding, passionate, fuck-me-Daddy, hard sex. Chris fucks my face, choking me until I gag repeatedly. I keep my eyes on his. They are hooded while his hands grip my hair for further control.

Gabriel fucks me ferociously from behind. Slamming his hips against my backside at the most perfect angle and hitting all the right spots. His hands grip my waist tight and I hope he leaves marks on me that last for days. I love seeing his love decorating my skin. Loud moans come from both men. I fucking own this moment and I never want it to end.

I allow my eyes to wander for only a second and I melt further. We beautifully display our shadows against my bedroom wall. Two fine and fit-as-fuck men railing me, making my dreams come true. And just as I am about to wish for *it*, it happens. They both release their grip on me and connect hands above.

An Eiffel Tower.

Then, just as I'm about to come. The dream abruptly ends. My body jolts, sweat dripping down my face and between my exposed breasts. And just because I hadn't come in my dream, it doesn't mean it hasn't happened in real life. I pull my fingers out from between my legs. They are moist, sticky, and covered in my release.

Shit.

Looking around, I'm alarmed to find my bedroom light on. I startle to see Fallon hunched over my bed frame at the foot of my bed. She's doing her labor breathing exercises. Crap, her water must have broke. She's come to get me, because I am part of her birthing plan.

Then my eyes widen in horror as laughter follows. Merrick. And standing in front of him is Hails, whose eyes are being covered by his hands.

Slowly, my head turns, utterly horrified. Gabriel is leaning up next to me, a giant shit-eating grin greeting me. "Care to share with the class?"

The E...

Wait. I have a song to reference too. Merrick isn't the only one allowed to compare his *boo*, pun intended, to a sick beat.

Okay. Here we go.

How come every time you come around, my London Bridge wants to go down? This song was absolutely written about Gabriel and I. And anytime I see his cock twitching, which happens every time I am in my man's presence. I bit my lip at the memory of his cock hitting it so perfectly. Just call my baby Captain Hook.

Fuck. I need to masturbate. Now, go pester someone else. I need my alone time.

Blow Me, A Port Canyon Chronicle - Coming When It Comes.
The En...

Merrick

No. don't you fucking dare close this book yet. Because I'm not calling her mom! Or mommy! Absolutely fucking not.

Fallon

Leave them alone, Merrick, please. These poor folks have put up with your antics for as long as I have. Give them a break. Let it breathe. And I'll give you a blow job for being such a good boy for me. Then, I'll let you suck on my succulent breasts. I know you love how my milk tastes. Don't you, baby?

Merrick

You are so sexy when you talk dirty to me, my hottie naughty slut. You had me at blow job.

Later, fuckers. Now, my stupid fucking girl, get on your knees and worship the cock that changed your life.

THE END.

Acknowledgments

Thank you for jumping back into Port Canyon with me! Without your love & support I wouldn't be able to do what I love each day, and for that, I am so grateful. Thank you!!

Nicole, because to use your full name makes me happy. When life gets stressful, we bring up torts and cheesecake to make us smile. You inspire me. You push me. You make me so fucking proud to call you my friend! My Fellow Libra, always!

To the Twisted Fiction family, thank you for giving me the push I needed to finally tell this story and put it out into the world.

Kata, Swizzle, Lucy, NJ, Rumi, Meme Lord and Amy. Thank you for helping me on this super secret mission. A select few knew I was doing this. One, because I wanted it to be a surprise. Two, worry and doubt. Merrick and Ghost Dick is my most beloved book and I didn't want to let anyone down or to disappoint.

The pressure to get this story right weighed on me

for two years. I hope you all enjoyed and that it lived up to the excitement around it. If not, that's okay too. I stayed true to Harper and her journey, and I loved every moment of it.

xx

Kins

About the Author

Kinsley is a Canadian, Dark Romance Author who dabbles in Taboo, Forbidden, Paranormal, Sarcastic Banter, Erotic Horror and is currently in her Dark RomCom Era. When she isn't plotting her next twisted book or watching true crime docs with her cat, you can find her napping, scrolling, or listening to Taylor Swift & Sleep Token.

Make sure you follow Kins on her socials and sign up for her newsletter to see what is coming next!

authorkinsleykincaid.com

Also by Kinsley Kincaid

FORBIDDEN

Let's Play (Archived)

Within the Shadows

Lessons from the Depraved

Haunted by the Devil; The Devil's Society

Sinner; The Devil's Society

Homecoming; The Devil's Society

Unholy; The Devil's Society

Sweet SIN Slaughterhouse; The Devil's Society

Beautiful Nightmare; English & German

The Adventures of Ruth & Martha

Reckless; The Devil's Society - Coming 2026!

TABOO

Wrecked

Sutton Asylum; The Tortured Souls

Sick Obsession; The Tortured Souls

Dark Temptation: Part One

Ghost Dick; A Port Canyon Chronicle

Dark Temptation: Part Two

Lessons; An Extremely Fucking Taboo Extended Epilogue

Brothers Bond

Fuck Me Daddy; A Port Canyon Chronicle

Taboo can be found via the authors' website.

eBooks & Signed Book Shop

www.ingramcontent.com/pod-product-compliance
Lightning Source LLC
LaVergne TN
LVHW012042070526
838202LV00056B/5561